G000067251

Back Road

Chris Gill

Fisher King Publishing

Back Road
Copyright © Chris Gill 2013
ISBN 978-1-906377-58-8

Fisher King Publishing Ltd
The Studio
Arthington Lane
Pool-in-Wharfedale
LS21 1JZ
England

Cover design by Sam Richardson

For Fiona, Archie,
Mum, Dad,
Jo and Karen.

Chapter One

I've always wanted to achieve something really big. Not like earning loads of money or acquiring huge status in the pecking order. I mean like taking a stand against something abhorrent or despicable. Taking a stand and winning through. Winning to an extent which rights a wrong and puts it right permanently. And on a really big scale. Something which is recognised and lauded nationwide. Even worldwide. Like the new Nelson Mandela. Yes, that would be something else. You see, I can't deny it, there's an egotist inside me. I might even rival the vainest billionaire property developers. Only, as the new Mandela, I would be far superior to such rich boys because I would have achieved something fundamentally important. Something which really mattered, something which transformed thousands of lives. Perhaps I never cared about others at all. It was probably always about me.

The first teaching job I landed was only for two hours a week but it came by way of fluke and so I attached some kind of pre-ordained destiny to it. I was staying at this aspiring playwright's house, helping him stage his latest work, when he got a call from a woman he'd never met. She thought he might know someone who could run a writing course for people with mental health issues. He put her on to me and I toughed it out because it seemed like fate. It also felt like I was 'putting something back,' changing lives on some miniature scale, which was at least better than shovelling shit around a factory. I still had to shovel shit around a factory, but now I had my two hours of worthiness which pandered to my battered ego and soothed it. So I found more work running courses for the vulnerable. I run courses for the vulnerable you know. I might not be Mandela but look how worthy I am.

Five years into the new millennium I got a job at number 14, Back Road, teaching adults with learning disabilities, which allowed me to pack in my job at the factory. The benevolent funding this charity received financed a decent hourly teaching rate, and paid enough for me to rent a one bedroom flat up in the roof of an old converted black stone church. My own place for once. Independent, worthy, helper of the vulnerable. I might not have been saving the world, ridding it of a Stalin or a Pol Pot, but I was now making a positive contribution on my own terms. This pleased me and, for a while, I believed I would just amble along with a bit more contentment in my own conscience and self image. I never imagined that soon I would be taking a stand, as I'd always wanted to, but within the context of a run-down hall down some backstreet.

You could walk past 14, Back Road a thousand times and not notice it. A squat, square, red brick building with grubby PVC windows, frosted glass and broken roof tiles. The lack of care with which the building has been tended to may appear to hint at a dereliction of care within its walls, but this is not my experience. All the day's sessions, such as Art, Music, Card Making, Drama, are run simultaneously in the flakily painted main hall. And only flimsy concertinaed mobile partitions partially separate these activities, giving a sense of utter chaos to those unfamiliar with the place. Indeed, chaos does at times reign in these circumstances where activities and challenging personalities frequently clash. But move closer, push past the tangle, settle at a busy table and, amid it all, are priceless things.

A woman with severely limited mobility learning to use a camera for the first time, a man at last understanding what is meant by the question 'how old are you?', a woman with poor verbal communication playing the role of her favourite soap star and lapping up the applause. Little things they may seem, but for those achieving them they are moments of delight and the keys to long buried potential. For years marginalised, these adults come to a place where they are central and valued as individuals. And that is, of course, why I came to this place. As a teacher I too was valued and central, and my ego loved that.

The teachers at Back Road, I would say, are easily as individual as the students. Jessica is a divorcee and mother of three in her late thirties. She runs the computer courses and her natural state is to run around giggling like a girl and deflecting her troubles with laughter. She is seeing her support assistant, Billy. He is her counterpoint, a gentle giant with an accent as broad as his shoulders. He calms her when frivolity threatens to spill into recklessness. He is quiet, she is noisy. She dresses tastefully, he slumps in t-shirts. They balance each other and people smile at their blossoming love. Zebadee is the music man who has been seen bouncing along to rock and roll and sing-a-long tunes as if he does, in fact, move on an invisible spring. He is irretrievably addicted to caffeine, which may explain some of the bouncing, and heavily burdened by debt. At twenty nine I suspect there are times when he thinks he's a failure, given that success to him is a world tour playing to thousands. Zebadee is most definitely an egotist like me, I spotted him the moment he walked through the door, but he hides it when teaching through sheer enthusiasm for subject and students. It is when I talk face to face with him that I see his ego in twitches and flickers. He's been battered like me but, though he may think it's hopeless, he still harbours a dream to make some sort of huge impact.

I have found it harder to relate to some of my colleagues. They do everything professionally and thoroughly, they prepare into the early hours and immediately follow up less effective sessions searching for alternative approaches. Their paperwork is spotless and beyond the call of duty. I would say I admire such people, though I do so begrudgingly. I could never be like them because I want to be spontaneous. I'd like to view spontaneity as better, but I must admit that it can fall flat on its arse. Sometimes I'm left floundering (it's all right for Zebedee, he's got his songs) and that's when I wish I'd stayed in the night before, planned well, organised a back up activity. Though for some reason I can never do it. Too busy escaping responsibility in drink maybe, and the mostly misguided belief that I'm going to pull if I go round the bars and try to look smouldering. Perhaps I don't plan that well just because it's not too cool. I don't know. I'm such a kid.

Helen is more professional than anyone. At thirty two, some say she's in danger of becoming a spinster. She lives alone and dresses most conservatively. And, when I started at Back Road, she was the last person I could ever see myself working with on anything.

Chapter Two

One Monday morning, about an hour before classes started, we'd brewed up and a few of us were puffing away in smokers' corner. The smoke curled around our heads and the knobbly shapes of the art group's grotesque papier-mâché models, then floated away drowsily through the opened fire exit, pulling with it a faint whiff of caffeine and glue paste. Zebedee was there, living out his punk phase, stopping short of sticking safety pins through his eyebrows but definitely practicing his Sid Vicious snarl when he thought people weren't looking. Helen was checking the minutiae of her lesson plans, like a royal butler meticulously combing through menus for a State banquet. Jessica was snuggled up to Billy, his voluminous jumper making her all cosy. She was nuzzling against the softness like a sex kitten. They'd obviously been shagging in the last few hours, the bastards.

Dotted along the edges of the main hall were stacks of furniture commandeered from shut down offices or exhibition venue clear outs; piles of imperfectly fitting plastic chairs, warped tables nestling awkwardly together, the inadequate mobile partitions folded against each other like weathered decks of cards left over winter in a summerhouse. Banks of objects punctuated the room, as if expanding on a theme of building, of accumulation; percussion instruments rose in tangled towers from boxes, little transparent trays filled with bright sparkling shapes balanced on each other, faces of concentration or pride or modesty shone out achievement from framed photos accumulated on the walls in squares of nine and sixteen. And through the kitchen serving hatch, stacks of plates and cups, meshes of cutlery, all lined up dutifully, ready for break-time and cheap sandwich lunches.

Presently, we were joined by Back Road founder and manager, the indefatigable Margaret. She has a freakish drive for a woman of thirty let alone sixty, but her constant attempts to always progress and move things on were beginning to wear her down. Such efforts seemed to lack the vision they once had. I wasn't sure about her judgement anymore. She was starting to lose her touch and her response was to work harder, to claw away at the rock-face like a climber searching for diminishing footholds. As she sparked up I noticed how sunken the deep brown circles around her eyes seemed, and how the lines emanating like spokes from her smoker's mouth appeared so harshly scored. She looked as if she hadn't had much sleep. She'd probably been lying awake in the dark hours, tugging the nicotine into her blackened lungs, not giving a toss about her own welfare but worrying about the students' well being and the part she felt obliged to play in it all. Nevertheless, back then, at least it was still clear to us who was in charge of the whole shebang. Back then her eyes were still resolute. We listened as she began her 'start the week' bulletin.

"So, we have a dance teacher dropping in today. What does everyone think? I think it will be a fantastic opportunity for some of our learners. A healthier activity leading to a healthier lifestyle. You understand. These are the life skills we're trying to promote now. We need to get more learners off their, pardon me, arses. I mean some of them just sit around all day."

"That's only because some of them have no choice," Zebedee springs in with the balls to say what the rest of us were thinking.

Margaret glared icily at him. We waited for her to continue and, inevitably, were not kept waiting long.

"We must inject more energy into the lives of those in our care. They rely on us to help them fulfil their potential. The more active they are, the more they will achieve. The more energetic they are, the more chance they will have to grow."

"Not forgetting that most of our guys put loads of energy into the activities we do Already, of course. You don't have to bounce around the floor to be energetic," I said, slouching, dragging on a crumpled 'roll up.'

"Well of course I know that, Pete," she snapped. "All I'm saying is that dancing, facilitated by a trained dance teacher, would be a welcome addition to what we do already."

"That's hunky dory then. I'm only saying. As long as it doesn't undermine..."

"Undermine? Who said anything about undermining?"

This was not a good idea. My hangover was really starting to kick in and an argument was the last thing it needed. There was only one place in town which stayed open until the early hours on a Sunday night and that was Stanley's; a total dive with seedy dark corners, very cheap lager and a grubby dance floor to match the grubby clientele. My God, I was grubby that night. I'd timed a couple of trips to the bar to coincide with those of a lass who looked a bit peripheral to her friends. Somehow I sensed she might be more receptive to a rubbish opening gambit like "Hi, can I get that?" or "Hardly Stringfellows, is it?" Her mates all looked like the sort to draw a chat up line out of you just so they could laugh in your face. I stood at the bar and dragged up some drunken courage.

"Hardly Stringfellows, is it?" I said.

She laughed.

"You can get these if you want," she said, batting her eyelids and running her fingers very slowly over the hem of her very short skirt.

"Right. Oh, right. Um, what's yours?" I was shifting awkwardly in the half light, trying to look charismatic. Failing.

"Cider. Pint please."

"Two of those cheers, mate." I said to the barman, who'd seen it all before.

"Copycat," she said, smiling faintly.

When I passed her the golden-orange pint she held it in front of her cleavage, the bubbles speeding up in the direction of her full lips, the glow of the liquid dully lighting up her face. She flickered her eyes at me again and smiled widely.

"Cheers, darling."

And that was her parting shot. She was off across the dance floor to join her mates. I could see them pointing and laughing at me, with my ego around my ankles. I downed a couple more quickly, by which time I was steaming drunk and no longer cared. I knew I was sad, they knew I was sad, so fuck 'em. Might as well be John Travolta until chucking out time. Travolta minus the rhythm, timing, style, class. Partner! The only concessions I could claim to be making to Danny

Triviani were bags of enthusiasm and some tight trousers I'd bought, thinking they were going to shape my backside into a pert temptation for the ladies. When in reality all they were doing was acting as a nutcracker for my balls. Safe to say, I must have looked a proper tit. It was hardly surprising I was less than chuffed by this dance teacher revelation the morning after. Margaret dug into me again.

"No, Pete, this will not undermine anything. What do you mean by that?"

"I didn't mean..."

"I can sympathise with what Pete's saying though," this was Helen, looking up from her lesson plan, trying to view things objectively, professionally. "The extra noise and movement is bound to effect students' concentration in other classes. Remember, we only have these tatty old screens separating the sessions."

"Gonna make that much difference? Place is pretty chaotic already," said Jessica, tightening her lips to suppress a giggle.

"Cope wi' a bit more racket can't we, folks?" said Billy, his powerful hand under the table, gently squeezing his new sweetheart's thigh and drawing from her an involuntary pig's snort of mirth.

"Well thank you for that, Jessica," said Margaret. "Thank you, Billy. We work in chaos, don't we? That is the nature of our work, isn't it? Isn't that what makes us different? Makes us special? All of you are here for a very important reason. Because you can deal with it. Just remember that. Don't lose sight of it. Do you think it's every person who can handle such anarchy as is found within these walls? Well of course it's not. Your students need you, they rely on you, they look up to you. In the middle of all this chaos, and their own personal chaos, you give them order and purpose. You give them *inspiration*."

A huge throb of hangover pain boomed around inside my skull. I winced in dehydrated guilt, for Margaret still occasionally found the power to say the right thing in the right way. Dance lessons were upon us and we were the ones who could welcome them, embrace them, almost celebrate their arrival. And in those moments, as we digested these thoughts, dance lessons did arrive at 14, Back Road; Deborah Styles showed up.

It's difficult to remember what my first impression of her was. I had nothing against her then so I didn't take much notice. I just thought about the dancing creating more bedlam in a place already bursting with it. But when I saw her putting her head around the door, edging uncertainly into the room, I was struck by the stature more than the demeanour; very short, very stocky. Like a Tasmanian devil at scrum half. Her clothes were dull and plain, her hair flat and lifeless. If she was trying to appear unassuming she was certainly dressed for the occasion. But thinking about it, her appearance exclaimed 'Dance Teacher' about as much as my dancing had 'Travolta' the night before. If my name was Sherlock perhaps I would have had her down as a fraud from the start. But I'm Pete, wrapped up in my own ego, and people like her are extremely clever.

"Deborah! Welcome," said Margaret, rising to meet her, touching her shoulder.

"Hello, Margaret. Morning every... everyone. Oh dear, sorry, I'm a bit..." said Deborah, petering out, her tongue flitting nervously across her lips.

"Well don't be. There's nobody scary here. Perhaps our music man, when he gets out his 'Lovely Bunch Of Coconuts,' but that aside."

The anarchic Zebedee stood up, boinging up and down like Johnny Rotten.

"Oh, I've got a lov-er-ley bunch o' coconu-uts! God save the coconu-uts! Their hairy hard she- ells! Their sweet tasting mi–ilk! Oh God save the coconu-uts!" he screeched. Thankfully, refraining from hawking phlegm up from his guts and gobbing it on the floor.

Most of us laughed, even Helen smiled a bit. Deborah smiled nervously, then feigned to leave. Then she guffawed so loudly it shut us all up. At the time I thought she was laughing with us, at Zebedee. Now I know her I reckon she was drawing attention to her own little joke, as she saw it. Calculating how to create the perfect impression, cultivating a sense of wit and light-heartedness. Carefree, fun loving, unthreatening. Pretending to have second thoughts? Hilarious, Debs.

By the end of the week Deborah had run a couple of dance sessions without disaster and without standing on anyone's feet. Some of the students had stood on each others' feet, actions accompanied by a piercing yelp or lamentable wailing, which caused the occasional grumble in nearby sessions. But Deborah could not have been sweeter towards her new students or, indeed, her colleagues.

"Are you absolutely certain we're not being too rowdy? We can tone it down with the twiddle of a knob. Ooh, sorry, that sounded a bit rude!... Right, I'll stop laughing now. Get a grip, Deborah. But seriously, just give me a nudge if we take too much space. The last thing I want to do is encroach."

Chapter Three

That Friday night I was out eating tapas with Jessica and Billy. Billy stabbed his fork into a tiger prawn and said, "Impressed wi' our new dance teacher then are we, kids?"

"She's left an impression," I said.

"Whenever she sits down. Built like a bullock," offered Jessica.

Now Billy had lost control of the prawn which slipped from his mouth, slid down his chin and plopped back into the olive oil filled dish. The oil spattered across Jessica's crisp white top which now looked like an artist's impression of piss holes in snow. I could see the anger playing on her lips, but she controlled it almost as soon as it appeared and turned to him with an expression somewhere between admonishment and affection.

"Think your luck's in tonight, do you?"

"Bloody hell I'm... bloody hell I'm really sorry."

"I know. You'll pay."

"Course I will. I'll have it cleaned tomorrow."

"And you'll squirm," she said, tossing an olive into her mouth.

"Anything, anything. Whatever it teks..."

"Take me to Spain, then."

She was about to laugh. I could see it bubbling in her throat.

"Eh?" said Billy.

"I'm told Seville is beautiful. If a little pricey."

"Eh?" he said, one great hangdog expression suspended

from his chops.

We saw his face and collapsed into laughter. Jessica only regained some control when the waiter shot us a reproving look.

"Don't worry, Billy, darling," she said. "Know you're strapped for cash. Morecambe'll do for me. If you're with me. Making me happy? Mmm? Big boy?"

"Oh fuck off you two, can't you?" I said.

At that they turned towards me and we all cracked up, until the waiter politely asked us to stop disturbing the ambience. When it came to paying Jessica wanted to pick up the tab. I remember her being pretty insistent about it, her wide eyes facing down our protestations with serious intent.

"I can afford it, guys," she said, as the waiter set down the tab on the table, equidistant from the three of us. "Not totally dependent on you blokes."

"If you can just pop your card in, madam, and tap in your number," said the waiter.

"Think I can't pay my way do you, boys?" she said, shaking her head in mock disapproval as she punched in her pin.

It seemed to be taking a while for the transaction to be processed. Then it started to feel like too long. It made me think of an actress in an amateur production, when it looks like she's pausing for dramatic effect, until it gradually dawns on the audience that she's forgotten her lines. Jessica slowly turned to the waiter, as if he were her prompter off stage left.

"There appears to be a problem, madam," said the waiter.

Jessica stared up at him, searching his face for a different line, the one in the script.

"Rejected," said the waiter.

"But there's money in it," she said. "Sure there's still enough money in it."

"Rejected."

"No bother," said Billy, handing the waiter his own card in return for Jessica's.

"Sure there's still enough money in it."

"Jess, we'll speak to t' bank on Monday. Listen to me, Jess. Jess?" said Billy.

"If that bastard was paying the maintenance he should be..." she said, the line fading away.

It took Billy a few minutes to bring her back to us, the tension in her face slowly dissipating under his loving embrace. It was as if he was gently wrapping something precious. He spoke kind words to her. I think I heard her giggling again.

But as all this was happening my mood began to shift. There was no laughter left in me when it came to walking home alone, picking my way unsteadily through drunken youth at chucking out time. I was definitely pissed, although watching Jessica and Billy's love had lent me sobering thoughts. Once I'd dragged myself back into the flat in the roof of the old black stone church, I opened the low sloping skylight window, slunk into my armchair and stared out across the rooftops with a roll up between my fingers. Soon memory mingled and blurred with beer and I was back in New South Wales a long time ago.

I was picking ripe fruit from gnarled trees corkscrewing

out of the parched earth. And I was thinking, questioning, looking back at my life in cynicism and disappointment. The sun burned through the mesh of branch and fruit and into my eyes, showing me the light. And now I was walking amongst scorched barbecues into a campsite at twilight. There was Willemeke, sitting against the trunk of a baobab tree by a stream, smiling up at me like I was all she'd been thinking of that day. Precocious, enlightened, twenty one, from Amsterdam. And I could see her standing as I approached, walking towards me with her gracefulness, her gorgeous tits, her wavy auburn hair. I could feel her putting her soft arms around my neck and her gentle, firm lips kissing mine. She reached into the stream to pull me out a beer and we sat beneath the tree together. The twilight began to pick out the stars. Heaven embraced the earth.

Ouch! I was suddenly aware of being in the armchair again, the last embers of my roll up burning my lips as I took one last hard drag. I crushed it and cursed it into the saucer I'd been using as an ashtray. I scanned the roof tops through the window once more, trying to recapture the memory of Willemeke. Only now I was back in that provincial English town, before I'd decided to jack it all in for a ticket halfway around the world, the town where I'd been making steady progress for a young man. There I was kitted out in a suit every day, feeling safe, secure, ordinary, living off the approval of the neighbours. But now I was gelling my hair in the mirror, trying to get it to curve the right way. And now I had to get out, get away, escape, because everything suddenly felt like prison. They were all behind me in the mirror saying, "stick around for a bit, don't be rash, don't burn bridges, what's a couple more months to be sure?" But I was sure. I put down the gel and there I was in the mirror, shaving off all my hair, laughing like a maniac, elated, and I was sure. Cast iron solid steel certain.

In my armchair I rolled another cigarette and sparked up again, gazing dreamily at the silhouetted rooftops. And I was back with Willemeke, my mind blurring into thoughts of us drinking beer under a tree by a stream at twilight. She was passionately explaining stuff like communist ideology and how the dichotomy between romanticism and classicism could be bridged. How these ideas might offer solutions to society's ills of capitalism and greed and disillusionment. Nobody had ever talked to me about these things before. I fixed my stare upon her confident lips, everything she said seemed important. Everything seemed right. And now I had a big smirk on my face. She was making me smug.

"Yes that is so true," I said.

"And so many people are trying to get to the top of the mountain, but they're so obsessed with reaching it that they forget to enjoy the journey," she said.

"They miss out on so much."

"They don't see the world."

"It's like all my mates back home, following false dreams, living out empty lives, chasing money," I said.

"Maybe their lives aren't empty..."

"I pity them."

She stroked my face, caressed it, slowly kissed me.

"Maybe we're being too... what's the word? Judge..." she

said, looking, as if for the answer, into the moonlit stream.

"Judgemental?"

"Judgemental."

"No, we're not," I said. "You see, I agree with you. And I do pity them. I do."

I drained my beer and reached into the stream to pull out another. But she dipped her hand in too and firmly held my submerged wrist. She looked intently into my face, like she was searching to understand me. We sat motionless for a bit. Then she said, "Slow down, Pete. Slow down. Don't let life pass you by. Watch the sky now. Lie here with me. Look at the night now."

So we lay supine by the tree, her hand holding mine, our mouths silent. Our faces starlit. Our hearts at peace. For what might have been a long time, gazing at infinity. But there was still something at the back of my brain, niggling. And I couldn't let it lie for too long. I could never let it lie. It broke the peace, it shattered the moment. Our moment in the universe.

"What have I been doing with my life?" I said. "Wasting it away. I've got to *do* something. I've thrown away so much time."

I was like a teenager in a strop. One big kid. And the next day I walked away from her, with my dusty rucksack and my selfish sorrow. Intent on making up for lost time, wanting to make the world a better place. But not modestly and quietly. No chance. I had to be a world beater in the world of philanthropy. I had to change things big style and, of course, I wanted all the credit to boot. Egotist!

A cloud scudded above the rooftops, revealing the moon, letting it shine on me through the opened window. Since Willemeke, me and my ego had always made attempts at putting the world to rights. I was dreaming of this again now, slouched in my chair; completing my degree, signing up to political organisations, applying to work for unions, attending rallies. Going on marches, being swallowed up by the tumult, just another anonymous nodding head drowning in some futile political protest. And sitting there, pulling on my roll up, I knew exactly why I hadn't taken it any further. I wanted to be in the vanguard, didn't I? On the rostrum, up front on a majestic white charger. And I'd been a million miles from that, so what was the point? There was no glory in being just like all the other activists.

The evening's drinking and the weight of these memories were making me drowsy. My thoughts turned hazier but less troublesome. I was picturing Back Road and the people I'd been employed to help. I saw snippets, glimpses, perhaps just a smile or an appreciative word from a student, moments which had been enough to sustain me. Those small signs of fulfilment which proved I could help change lives. The meaning and purpose of it all which was finally with me now; the realisation that my life was worthwhile by actually starting to think of other people, instead of just myself.

I slipped towards sleep, as a seductive breeze blew through the skylight and kissed my cheeks. I sunk down into the armchair and my eyelids grew heavy. My vision faced towards a blurring image of an enlightened young woman with wavy auburn hair, stepping slowly away down a dusty track.

Chapter Four

A couple of months later we were deep in winter. It was a Saturday night and the mood was celebratory; Margaret's sixtieth birthday. A load of us had piled into a curry house, dashing sleet from coats, rubbing warmth into fingers, and dressed up a long table with helium balloons and rainbow streamers. Helen had arranged everything, needless to say most competently. She'd sorted the booking, confirmed it, reconfirmed it, collected our money for a present, purchased the gift, after extensive consultation with all contributors, and bought a card carrying a message which was appreciative without being too sentimental.

Around the table, our appetites left to feed tantalisingly on the smell of garlic and coriander drifting in from the kitchen, we waited for Margaret to show. I was sitting opposite Zebedee, who had somehow floated away from his punk frenzy and into the mellow world of Donovan. Yes, he was dressed in yellow. Except he looked more like an ice cream than a flower power man. Jessica and Billy, canoodling, were next to him. They were laughing at him, though only in a spirit of peace and love. If Donovan had been sitting opposite he'd have composed a belter. Zebedee turned to them.

"I'm not digging your vibe, guys," he said, lifting a flower from a vase on the table and trying to inhale its aroma deeply. Right up until the moment he realised it was plastic. He returned it and buried his head in a menu.

Between me and the place reserved for Margaret, at the head of the table, was Deborah. She was tittering away with us and, aside from touching my knee once or twice when trying to be funny, she was decent enough company for most of the evening. By then, I had a pretty good idea she was getting her feet well under the table with Margaret at Back Road, but I hadn't started seeing her as a threat. I could even have a laugh with her, then. Zebedee was still hiding behind his menu when she said, in a voice half singing:

"Zebedee? Oh, Zebedee?"

"Yeah, babe?" he said, peering around the laminated list.

She pointed at his creamy yellow shirt.

"Would you like a flake with that?"

And we all cracked up.

The clock on the wall, centred amid spiky golden sunbeams, showed that Margaret was twenty minutes late when she came through the door and approached our table. Deborah stood instinctively, immediately offering to hang her coat. For some reason Margaret had forgotten to put her hood up and sleet had pasted her hair to her scalp. She was wearing polka dot wellies, which looked like pathetic substitutes for a party frock. She didn't really seem into it but she went along with the "congratulations!" and birthday hugs before taking her seat at the top of the table.

The evening rattled along for a while, the place filling up with punters and chatter and myriad spices merging. Bottles of red wine punctuated the table and Margaret was sharing one with Deborah. I was already becoming interested in their relationship. They'd become close so quickly. Deborah, using kindness and wit, was trying to make Margaret smile. Margaret was having a shot at it but the corners of her mouth kept stopping just short of the points where a smile is natural; they stretched upwards and then appeared to teeter and retreat. She was certainly knocking back the vino. I was busy taking the piss out of Zebedee but, to my right, I caught the glint of light on a tipped wine bottle each time Deborah replenished Margaret's glass.

"What did Sid Vicious make of it though, man?" I said.

"Qu'est - ce que c'est?" Zebedee hazily replied.

"Waking up with burning josticks in his piercings?"

"To be hopes you haven't got a 'Prince Albert', lad!" said Billy.

Zebedee was taking himself far too seriously to find that one funny. He lifted his head and closed his eyes, as if to indicate that he was now way above such preposterous juvenility. It just made him look like a pompous dick though. At least Helen tried joining in. She asked Billy what a 'Prince Albert' was and, when Jessica whispered in her ear, her face turned scarlet.

"I think you've stumbled upon the quintessential identity crisis there, Pete," she said.

But somehow that statement sort of drew all the wind out of the humour. I caught myself looking at her, thinking, 'bloody hell, you're a barrel of laughs.'

Helen sipped slowly from a tall glass of water, Zebedee remained ludicrously aloof. Billy beamed like a gold counting giant, as Jessica giggled about 'Prince Alberts'. I noticed again the glinting wine bottle to my right. Only this time my attention was held for longer. I made out to be focussed on mopping my plate with a final chapatti, but kept sneaking a look at Margaret and Deborah. Margaret's eyes were glazed. It was probably the wine. And the alcohol seemed to have subdued her; she was face to face with Deborah but she wasn't saying much. She had her head tilted most of the time as she rested her chin on her palm. Deborah mirrored the head tilt in an attitude which portrayed sympathy. Then she put her hand on Margaret's forearm, gently gripping, like she was trying to squeeze something out of her. This appeared a touch too much for Margaret who stood abruptly and walked a wobbly course to the toilets. Around the table heads turned and conversations faded.

"What's up, Deborah?" I said.

"She says she's all right."

"I'll check she's ok," said Helen, half standing.

"I'll go," said Deborah, making a beeline for The Ladies.

Helen sat back down. We rested forwards on our elbows, knitting tighter together.

"Can you sense her aura, people? I'm getting some nasty vibrations," said Zebedee.

"Quit the masquerade now, can't you?" I said, irritably.

We threw a few theories around about the psychological effects of landmark birthdays, winter blues and bad hair days. But by the time they returned to the table, Deborah unnecessarily guiding Margaret by the elbow, the majority held the cause to be too much of the red stuff. I didn't have a clue what the crack was.

Deborah held Margaret's chair for her, pushing it in slightly as she sat down. She shrugged her shoulders in response to our questioning faces. Then she sat beside

Margaret and assumed an attitude of concern once more. Margaret stared at the unfinished mess of curry and torn naan bread on her plate.

"So Margaret, was there a heavy bell tolling outside your window when you awoke as a sexagenarian this morning?" I said, immediately regretting the clumsy effort at humour. It was right up there with some of my chat up lines. It felt like someone had opened the restaurant door at that moment and gusty winds were cart-wheeling tumbleweeds across our table.

Margaret stayed dead still, her stare stuck on her plate. Then, by degree, she started shaking. Almost imperceptibly at first but, as she interlocked her fingers and the ageing knuckles whitened, the shakes visibly shuddered her. And a silent crying seeped from her deeply set eyes. Deborah moved in closer, laying a comforting arm around her shoulders.

"Now what's the matter, darling?" she asked, as everyone else awkwardly shifted.

Margaret sucked in the air, steeling herself to face us and just come out with it.

"I'm sorry but I received some awful news yesterday. I don't know how to say this but... after you'd all gone home, the board of trustees and myself held a meeting at Back Road with our main benefactors. And the upshot is that they are withdrawing all their funding of community projects. I'm afraid that includes charities like ours. And that amounts to nearly half of what we need to run our courses; to rent Back Road, pay the bills, pay your wages. I'm sorry, I'm so sorry..."

Upon this devastating revelation Deborah at once

withdrew her arm from Margaret. You'd think she'd been stung. I thought about that a lot afterwards. The rest of us were gazing into our curries, as if blends of tarragon and chilli could be read like tea leaves. Margaret was crying again but her anger was beginning to fight it.

"What's going to happen to our students if we have to close?" she said. "What are they going to do all day? Stay at home doing jigsaws?"

"Can't you persuade these benefactors to change their minds?" said Jessica.

"What do you think we tried to do?"

"Can't just give up on it."

"Give up?" said Margaret, glowering.

I thought Deborah, new bosom buddy, might have stepped in then to defend her. But nothing. She'd kind of sunk into her chair silently, like a spy. We'd all taken a slug to the guts though, so nobody spoke for a minute. And it must have been this group response which sparked off the leader in Margaret again, the responsibility she felt towards us, the care, the altruism, the love. She soaked up her tears in her serviette and sat up tall.

"Ok now. Come on, you lot. Isn't this a party? I certainly haven't given up on getting funding elsewhere. In fact, I have heard the council may be starting to fund supported learning courses. Helen, have you heard anything?"

"Yes they are. And all our students are on the spectrum of learners they're looking to target," said Helen, getting into her stride. "I've researched this actually and..."

"You see, everyone," exclaimed Margaret, arms aloft,

fingers splayed. "*Helen* agrees with me. *And* she's researched it! How much reassurance do you need?"

A couple of people did their best and had a laugh at that. But to me it sounded like Margaret was trying to reassure herself. For the rest of the evening most of us escaped in drink and, eventually, things showed a semblance of what they'd been before Margaret arrived; a celebration, only slightly slurred. I was pretty tanked by the end of the night and getting home was a bit sketchy. Although there was one clear memory from the latter stages of the evening still knocking around inside my head. It was the image of Deborah Styles' hand, back around Margaret's arm, gently gripping.

Chapter Five

By the time winter was fading and white and purple crocuses lined the roadsides, we were all feeling the pinch. Our hourly teaching rate had been cut by a third. That was nearly a half! And rent collectors remained heartless bastards. Moreover, such a savage saving notwithstanding, Back Road's future continued to seem like a pissed tightrope walker with a distaste for safety nets. Without local authority funding the place looked finished. Margaret, increasingly panicked, had been in negotiations with the council since the week after her birthday. And still nothing conclusive. For me it wasn't just about keeping a job and paying the rent though; I'd been watching Deborah Styles ever more closely.

One afternoon the mobile partitions were up and we were cracking on with our sessions. My Storytelling class was in the centre of the hall, surrounded on all sides. I heard Jessica behind me, fluttering excitedly between computers, doubtless inspiring students with her energy. In front, through a gap in the partitions, I saw Helen teaching Textiles. Quietly, she was helping her learners make a patchwork quilt. Her calm face watched over everyone, allowing them space and time to explore texture and colour. I always get a pang of envy watching that kind of serenity. Zebedee was somewhere off to my right, playing 'music from around the world' on the guitar, his students accompanying him with shakers they'd made. There was plenty to distract me and, when Zebedee spun a CD of sitar playing, my mind flirted with travel memories. But what really kept diverting my attention was happening behind the screen to my left, where Styles was directing show rehearsals for a musical.

In Storytelling, we were developing protagonists for our stories using the 'hot seating' exercise, in which students sit in the middle of a circle on the 'hot seat' answering questions about their imagined character. When Marilyn's turn came she was in a highly charged state of enthusiasm. She'd been right up in my face about ten times already.

"Is it my turn yet? Is it my turn? When's it my go? Is it my turn? Do I know you, love? What's your name? Is it my turn now?"

"Very soon, Marilyn, very soon."

"Yes. Yes. Thanks, love."

After exchanges like this Marilyn would sink forlornly back into her seat in the circle, until some minutes later when, having forgotten it all, she'd be up to my face again, just about nose to nose.

"Is it my turn yet? Do I know you, love?"

Now she was finally in the hot seat, with her forty year old countenance framed in a bowl cut and her grey tracksuit bottoms two inches too short. She was shuffling around on her backside so much with the excitement of it all, you'd think the seat was literally hot.

"Right, Marilyn's turn," I said, joining the circle. "Are you ready, Marilyn?"

"Ready, ready."

"Good. Okay, concentrate. I'll take notes for you."

"Oh, brilliant, love. Brilliant!" she shouted, tucking her fists tightly under her chin, trying to control herself.

"Right, we'll be asking questions about the character you're thinking of, so you can learn more about him or her for your story..."

"Yes. Come on, everyone, ask me. Ask me."

"Has anyone got a question about Marilyn's character?" I said, looking around the circle of students.

Tracey stood, walked up to Marilyn, placed her hands on her shoulders and seriously stared into her eyes.

"Is it a man, Marilyn? Is it? Is it a man?" she asked.

Marilyn, deadpan, looked back at Tracey for a few seconds, before replying like an informant with a whisper too loud.

"No, it's a woman."

"Oh," said Tracey, pensively stroking her chin as she walked back slowly to her chair.

"Does she have a job?" asked Ronnie, in his Status Quo tour T. shirt.

"Yes, yes, yes. She's got a job! She's got a job!" said Marilyn at full throttle, bouncing up and down on the hot seat with the thrill of it all.

"Okay, everyone, a good start," I said. "So far, we have a woman with a job. But does that sound like an interesting character for a story?"

Then Styles' voice cut in from the session beside us. I'd been trying to ignore it, as it knocked against the partitions, but it was too sharp now. It penetrated.

"Diane, am I wasting my time with you? Sometimes I feel I am. I won't tell you again. Our musical is going to be a *medley* of songs. You might have seen 'Annie' about a thousand times, but we are not doing every song from that show. I know it's hard for you, but can you please try to understand?"

Why was she talking to her students like that? Had she actually worked with vulnerable people before?

"I think she's an interesting character," said Ronnie, back in Storytelling.

"Sorry?" I said.

"A woman with a job. That's interesting," he said, sprawled on his chair.

"Why?"

"Because, in the olden days, a lot of women didn't have jobs."

"That's true, Ronnie. Is your story set in the olden days though, Marilyn?"

"What, love?" asked Marilyn, looking like she'd just returned from a daydream.

"The character you're thinking of? The woman with a job? Did she work a long time ago, or is she working now?"

"Oh, she's got a job now. She's just got a new job!" she said.

Styles cut in again from behind the partition.

"So, everyone, just sit quietly and listen please... Good. You see you *can* do it. Now, this is the running order I've decided on for our medley of songs and dances from musicals. 'Oh What A Beautiful Morning,' 'Food Glorious Food,' 'All That Jazz,' 'Tomorrow,' from 'Annie,' just for you, Diane. Will that suffice? Mmm? Can you cope now? Good. And, finally, I will be performing the song 'Cabaret' for the grand finale, the big finish! Everybody happy? You just need to follow my direction at all times. Remember, I am in charge."

My mind had wandered away from the Storytelling session and drifted over the partition into Styles' world of musicals. It was watching her, wondering what made her tick: Did she need to be so patronising? Why did she want some of the glory for herself? Why did she have to emphasise being in charge all the time? Where did this need for control come from? If I was her director, what would I think her motivation was? And what effect was her approach having on her students?

"What's her job, Marilyn?" asked Julie, in Storytelling.

"Nice one, Julie," I said, focussing on my work again. "The answer to that question could make Marilyn's character much more interesting."

Marilyn had a big grin on now.

"Shovelling horse muck!" she exclaimed, clenching her fists, as if in victory.

When everyone had stopped laughing, I turned to her.

"Marilyn, haven't you just got a part-time job where you go horse riding?"

"Yes. Yes I have."

"Are *you* the character in your story, Marilyn?"

"Yes I am. It's me! It's me!"

But then I found myself listening in on Styles' session once more. Margaret must have walked in from the office.

"Deborah, can I have a word?" she asked.

And all I could think about was why Margaret kept wanting a word with Styles?

Chapter Six

We were well into spring when we heard that Margaret, Styles increasingly at her side, was close to securing new funding for Back Road from the council. She looked whacked but she still had enough fight in her. She must have been driven on by thoughts of what would happen to other people if Back Road collapsed. We'd been told that if a deal was finalised the council would fund some Back Road courses at close to the previous, higher, hourly teaching rate of pay. *Some* of the courses. The rest would still have to be paid for by Back Road and its remaining benefactors. And, with money still tight, these courses would be funded at the much lower hourly teaching rate currently in operation. One third off. It felt like being a discount item in the sales.

I remember the day I started thinking the shit was really going to hit the proverbial. It was lunchtime and students were variously occupied in the main hall. Some flicked through magazines and pointed at the famous, some sat with their noses pushed up close to computer screens, some laughed, some dozed, some danced. Helen walked purposefully in from the office carrying an immaculate course folder, neatly ordered with beautifully designed session plans and worksheets.

"Pete, the photocopier's free for you now," she said.

"Ta. Is Deborah in...?"

But her ponytailed head was already buried in her folder, visualising the afternoon session, making contingencies for the unexpected.

When I walked into the office Margaret was sitting there hunched over piles of papers, thumbing through them fitfully, slamming down staplers and rulers. And Styles was hanging around, a portrayal of worry lining her face. At the edge of the room I started photocopying, trying to look busy but with my attention fixed on the women.

"It's here somewhere," said Margaret, impatiently.

"Of course you're right, Marge," said Styles, lacing her voice with sympathy.

"I put it here. I know I did."

Styles turned to me, shrugging, hands upturned, highlighting for me our manager's unnecessary anxiety and the need for her own kindly intervention. She moved to her, a heavy exhalation of concern escaping through her thin lips. She placed her palm firmly on Margaret's shoulder and squeezed slightly.

"Margaret, Margaret, Margaret," she said.

"I put it down here somewhere, I'm sure of it. Am I going mad?"

"Now don't be silly, Marge."

"Am I losing my mind?"

"Marge, listen to me. Calm yourself."

"Where's it gone?"

"I'm here, aren't I?" said Styles, like a mother picking up her fallen child.

"Yes... yes you are, Deborah," said Margaret, pushing a hand through her hair and looking up at Styles from her swivel chair.

"So we'll find it together won't we, darling?"

"Yes, yes, of course we will."

"I'm sure we are just about to find it," said Styles, methodically searching.

"Where is the bugger?"

"I can sense it in my water."

Now I'd pressed the wrong button and jammed the photocopier. It moaned. Then Margaret at last found the document. She waved it above her head triumphantly.

"Halleluuuujaaahh!" she said, passing the document to Styles.

"Now did I not tell you we'd find it, Margaret?"

"You did, Deborah, you did."

"Did I not say there was nothing to worry your little self about?"

"You did, Deborah. Pete, can Deborah just copy this please? We can work off the photocopy and put the original away for safe keeping. With my scatter brain I think it's the sensible option. Don't you, Deborah?"

"With your scatter brain I think it's the only option," said Styles, before guffawing like a cartoon villain.

I caught Margaret looking askance at her. I think she was still trying to weigh her up. But then she fell in with the laughter. Perhaps it was easier that way, to accept rather than question. She'd asked too many questions lately, of those she'd once trusted. Maybe the answers were too painful and now she again needed someone she could trust. Despite suspicions, she needed someone to shore her up, give her back some strength, make things all right.

"Is that all right with you, Pete? Yeah?" asked Styles.

"Sorry?" I was confused. My brain seemed to have jammed like the photocopier. I was trying to compute just what was going on here.

"To copy this document a moment. It is quite important. Fine and dandy with you, Pete? Yeah? Only three sheets. Then it's all yours. Sorry to encroach but ..."

"Do it," I said.

I ripped the stuck paper from the machine, pressed the reset button and stood back. She approached, holding the document reverentially, as if it were made of gold leaf. As she turned it to face downwards I caught a good glimpse. The document was on the council's headed paper and there were a couple of subheadings, 'Course Requirements' and 'Course Aims.'

"These the courses the council's funding, Margaret?" I said, turning my back on Styles.

"More guidelines really. Of the sort of thing they're prepared to fund."

"Right. And..."

"Don't worry, Pete, you'll get something with them," she said.

"And everyone else?"

"A man of your calibre."

"And everyone else?"

"We have to draw up proposals which meet their guidelines first," she said.

"We? And who's we?" I said.

She tried casting that icy glare at me but it melted too easily now. She averted her eyes. She was losing her conviction. I turned to Styles, my own eyes frozen. She looked up from the copier, bold as you like.

"Nearly done!" she said.

Chapter Seven

At half four I walked into the 'Cock and Bottle' with Zebedee, Jessica and Billy. It's the kind of pub where you'd expect to find a spittoon in the corner. Whenever we go in there's always this old geezer sitting on a bar stool where the bar meets the wall. He leans into the right angle and angles his chest so the light makes the row of medals on his blazer gleam. I still haven't worked out whether he's a genuine war veteran. Most frauds make loads of claims attempting to persuade you of their stories' authenticity. I've never heard this bloke mention the war. But then his collection of medals looks so eclectic you'd swear it had been gathered from a series of car boot sales.

"Young 'uns in agin, Harry," he said to the barman.

"Eh up, Pop," said Zebedee, who'd recently been re-energised by a country and western vibe.

"Cheeky bastard."

"Come off it, Pop. It's a term of endearment."

"It's an Americanism," I said.

"New Orleans, Memphis; Tennessee, Sweet Home Alabama. 'Pop' is a term of endearment," said Zebedee, bouncing up to the bar. "Now what can I get ya'all?"

"Thought you were skint, Zeb," said Jessica.

"Nope."

From the inside pocket of his blue suede jacket he produced a wedge of twenties, folded once and held together with a gold band the shape of a squashed bicycle clip. I had a good idea where he'd got the twenties, but the gold band?

Perhaps it was a bicycle clip and he'd had it gold plated. Anything to make an impact, to be talked about. I almost expected him to strike a match on the sole of his cowboy boot and magic a half-chewed cheroot from behind his ear.

"Zebedee!" screeched Jessica.

"What?"

"Another loan, is it? You crazy? Never paid the last one off already. Raving mad. You can see people about this sort of thing, you know. It's like a condition. Something's flipped. Heading for trouble, Zeb. No! Big big trouble. It's a spiral. Soon you'll never get out of it. Debt over your head for the rest of your life. It'll rule your life. I know about this, Zeb. Ever meet my ex? Do you actually know what he's doing to me and my kids? His own children? Well... I'm telling you... Ruin you! That's what it'll do!"

She was digging her nails into her palms. I'd never seen her like this before. Billy was dumbfounded. He enveloped her in his massive arms, as he often did. But this time confusion and shock defined his face. I tried to catch his eye but he was somewhere else, staring at the floor.

"Hey cool it, honey pie," said Zebedee. "Loans are like my second wage. You know that. It's the way I am, that's all. I am what I am, as the old song goes. Listen, Sugar, don't lose sleep. You reckon I'll be losing sleep?" Zebedee stroked her hair and then moved in beside the old man. "Usual's all round, guys and gals? Rack 'em up, then."

The three of us moved to the pool table as Zebedee wantonly bought a full round on borrowed money. It's so much more fun for him that way. It makes him feel reckless and daring, like his heroes. Even though most of his heroes spend their time in tax havens, sitting on fortunes. Of course he knows this. He's not stupid. But he also knows about the image and the fantasy and they seem so much more relevant to him than the reality. He was making the old man laugh now. As I filled the black plastic triangle with pool balls I looked across the lowly lit green baize and watched him larking about. God knows what he was saying, but he kept bending over the old man's ear and whispering, then standing up straight, tittering to himself. The old man didn't make any noise, but his whole body shook and his medals glinted and glistened and danced on his chest.

When I'd set up the pool table Billy was still trying to soothe Jessica's mood with soft words and gentle kisses. Zebedee walked over carrying a tray of drinks.

"Doubles?" I asked, chalking my cue tip.

"Jess and me," said Billy.

"Naturally," I said. "Hustler, you up for it?"

"You kidding?" said Zebedee, planting the drinks on faded beer mats.

We played some frames and lit up the jukebox with Otis Redding and Johnny Cash. A couple of pints in and the late April sun had dipped into the pub's dirtied, dusty window frames. I'd started to emulate some of Zebedee's cockiness by shielding my eyes from the sun with one hand and playing shots with the other but I was becoming irritable. At one point I missed the white ball, nearly ripping the cloth with my cue.

"Steady, man. This loan won't stretch to a new table," said Zebedee.

"You are all aware of what Styles is up to, aren't you?" I said.

"She's like buffed up glass," Billy winked at Jessica.

"Can see right through her," she said, robotically.

"Bum! Bum!" said Zebedee.

"You can forget the Basil Brush impressions, Zeb," I said. "It's not kids' stuff this, you know."

"All right. All right. Chill ..."

"Chill? What, like you? And get ourselves into deeper and deeper shit?"

"Eh, Pete, hold up..." said Billy.

"Billy, this is serious," I said.

"What's happened now?" said Jessica, suddenly focussed on me.

It hadn't taken much to darken the mood. By then I was seeing Styles for what she was and, though my colleagues were more sceptical, they had started to meet my concerns with increased interest. She was, at the very least, making them uneasy. Within minutes, having abandoned the game, we were circled around a rickety table, leaning inwards like conspirators.

"Look, Margaret's started wandering around like a puppet," I said. "And you know who's working the strings. This lunchtime I'm in the office and she's flapping about looking for a memo from the council. Who's there to pick up the pieces? Exactly. I tell you, beyond belief. She'll help her out because she's vulnerable, she'll offer a shoulder because she's cracking up and then, whack, she'll take a slice. I'm telling you, a slice of whatever she can get for herself. That's her criteria. You do know that, don't you? There's Margaret, devoted to everyone but herself, and there's that mercenary bastard abusing her kindness. Using her completely. I thought we were at Back Road to improve the lives of others, not to use the place for our own ends, our selfish ambitions. Not to think only of ourselves and what we can get out of it. We need to do something."

"What happened?" said Jessica.

"And I'm not happy about how she treats the students sometimes either. How she talks to them. Like they're children. Patronising cow. How is that building them up? Giving them confidence? Encouraging them to be independent? It says everything about her attitude towards our students, that does. What she really thinks of them. We need to keep an eye on that too. I actually think it's disgusting, the way she talks to our guys."

"I agree with you," said Jessica. "But what happened in the office, Pete?"

"So I'm in there using the copier and Margaret's lost this letter from the council and there's a big panic on. Rulers, rubbers, staplers flying about. Post-it notes fluttering like confetti, except there's no celebration. Poor Margaret. The world's going to cave in unless she finds that edict from her new masters. And there's Styles offering reassurances, clocking up points and depositing them in her memory bank. To be withdrawn when favours need repaying. Anyway, at last, Margaret finds it."

"What did it say? Did you find out what it said?" asked Jessica, alert as prey.

"It was guidelines for the courses."

"What courses?" said Billy and Zebedee.

"The sort of courses the council is prepared to fund."

"When was Margaret going to tell us about these guidelines, exactly?" said Jessica.

"When she's drawn up some proposals with Styles, maybe," I said.

"What's *she* doing helping Margaret with proposals?" said Jessica, her calves pushing her chair backwards as she stood, making it scrape angrily across the worn wooden floor.

Chapter Eight

The next day bank holiday weekend began and I wanted to escape. I dug out the muddied old rucksack I'd used in my travelling days from under the sink. I ran my thumb over the reddish ochre smudges and pictured the infinite flat expanse of the Outback and the translucent heat of the Rajistani desert. The days of shimmering promise. Then there was someone in 'Residents' Parking' beneath my window, bringing me back prosaically home.

"Out my bloody space!"

I stuffed the rucksack with crumpled clothes, slung it across my shoulder, descended three flights of stairs and jumped into my tired, decayed eleven hundred. I can't remember much about the journey. Occasionally I noticed a distinctive looking vehicle pulling out in front of me and then, a couple of miles later, I'd be thinking 'where's that lorry gone?' 'what happened to that tractor?' I had no recall of these vehicles turning off. My car was like my time machine transporting me back to yesterday, when I should have stepped in and stopped Styles exploiting Margaret. The heat of the Rajistani desert had blown across the oceans and was now sitting in my head in a simmering, stewing anger.

I snapped out of it when a ram lost its footing and tumbled into the road in front of me. The brakes screamed and the car juddered to a harsh halt. I slowly uncurled from an instinctive ball, by which time the ram was standing and staring up at my windscreen. Our eyes met. But the love was lacking. He rammed the front grill like a rhino playing dodgems. The car juddered again, its rusting metal mournfully creaking. The ram turned, leapt up the grass verge onto the dark moorland heather and was away. I rested my forehead on the steering wheel and felt a confusion of emotion rising in my throat. I swallowed it down and stilled myself a while. Looking up again, I scanned a familiar moorland landscape.

I parked the car, pulled a thick coat from my rucksack and began walking along the high road which bent and wove across a valley top. To my right the earth fell away sharply where, dropped by ancient glaciers, jagged boulders jutted upwards to pierce the rich browns and luxuriant greens of spring. A thin stream, perhaps a hundred feet down, created a fissure of glinting sunlight in the valley bottom. The sky was as clean as glacial waters, yet a rapier wind stung at my face as I pushed my way up the valley.

I soon arrived at a rarely trodden pathway, as narrow as a man's boot, to the right of the road. I followed its snaking zigzags a short distance down the valley side until I reached two huge blocks of square rock. Between the rocks is a space from which I can observe the valley for miles in both directions. I go to this place when I'm low. Something about it holds a perfect sense of tragedy. Indeed, it is so precipitous there that one slip means death. Yet tragedy always mutates from life and hope, and that day a lone sparrow hawk, battling against the gusts, balanced on the wind near the edge of my reach.

I watched it, the air blurred my eyes and the bird became the one in India which had looked out for me. The one which symbolised a dream to stem the misery of the suffering millions beneath its wings. The messenger telling me to fight injustice and cruelty as though I'd been chosen. The one which convinced me I *had* been chosen. Egotist! In Delhi it had soared above my crumbling rooftop sleeping places, in Kerala it had rested beside me on the prows of slow Backwater boats, before me in Varanasi it had dipped and tilted low above the holy waters of The Ganges. And it was still with me. Except now it mocked my failings and ridiculed my futility. Then an image of Styles pushed its way into my head, looking up at me from that photocopier, bold as bollocks, "nearly done!", "nearly done!", taking the piss. I was convinced she was mocking me too. She was obviously after snatching a couple more highly paid courses for herself, but it wasn't the money which got to me most. The one place which had given me a shot at some proper altruism and there she is using it just to grab what she can. We were supposed to be there for the good of others for fuck's sake! And what was she doing? Pretending to help those less fortunate, but really using them for what she could get out of it. I could see it. It was right there in my face. I knew what it was like to want to use others, didn't I? To gain recognition for myself? That was me before I started at Back Road. The sparrow hawk raised a wing, like a fighter jet at the conclusion of a mission, and allowed the wind to carry it off back down the valley. I watched it shrink and disappear.

The wind was stronger now. Repeatedly buffeting my coat, it began to drag me from self pity towards a strange kind of exhilaration. The danger of the place was part of it but the safety of the nook between the rocks equally so. It was like being a child again, snug under the duvet as the storms raged. Knowing I was safe, whilst feeling the danger so close. So close that I could draw it into my bedroom with one mad hurl of a stone through glass. Not wanting to do it, but wanting to. The power of having the choice, but the doubt about what I would choose.

It was lunchtime when I drove into the remote village a mile or so further up the valley. High up on the valley side, it is overlooked by a medieval church which, from a distance on misty mornings, can appear to float above the community. And here religion is central. The small population always fills the church on Sundays and absences are still frowned upon, as if the last fifty years had never elapsed. There are no street lights and the road stops at the church. Beyond lie miles and miles of unpopulated moorland crisscrossed only by tracks for ramblers and horse riders. In this village it is possible to imagine that modernity, its pressures, demands, guilt trips, multimedia, justice, injustice, selfishness, vanity, altruism, fame, is mere myth.

The Crown pub stands just down the road from the church. It always reminds me of how my granddad's house used to look; brasses hanging everywhere, furniture polished smooth through decades of use, china decorated with mock oriental flora. After booking two nights' bed and breakfast I dumped my rucksack on the bed, where a Bible had been placed at an angle on the pillow, and went downstairs to the taproom. I sat on a barstool and ordered a pint from the landlord, a huge Santa Claus figure with a big round belly and a beard as thick as a thatched roof. This nicotine, whisky-stained phenomenon has a muffling effect on his voice, making listeners feel lucky to catch half of the words in each sentence. Nevertheless, with eyes twinkling and jolly laughter shaking the optics, his sentiment is always clear.

"Muffle muffle muffle wind up muffle backside ho ho. Muffle," he said.

"Beautiful day though," I said.

"Not had a muffle muffle for a bit now."

"Really?"

"Scarcely a muffle," said the landlord.

"Is that good?"

"Muffle yer blessings, lad. Ho ho."

"True. Can you put another half in there please?" I said.

"Pleasure. Grouse season'll muffle muffle muffle."

"The glorious twelfth, eh? Cheers."

"They'll muffle muffle in their finery. Ho ho. Mark my muffle."

"I'll bet that boosts the old coffers."

"Muffle," said the landlord, pensively stroking his magnificent beard.

"How is business?" I asked.

"Need more weddings."

"Well, with the church next door..."

"Ho ho ho ho ho!" he roared, big belly wobbling.

"What?"

"Oh, I'll tell you this muffle. Hilarimuffle."

"Go on," I said, resting my elbows on the bar, leaning towards him.

"This couple get muffle muffle, right?"

"Erm... right."

"And so reception's here. Hee hee hee."

"Go on."

"And the groom's muffling his speech. In front of all the muffles, right?"

"Yeah."

"And he thanks her parents and muffle muffle muffle muffle..."

"Yeah? Yeah?"

"And so he... hee hee hee ho ho ho!"

"Come on..."

"He gets to the best muffle and says: 'And muffle I'd like to thank my best man for servicing my wife for the past six months!"

"No!"

"Yes! Yes! Yes!" said the landlord, cracking up, his belly like blancmange.

"And he's gone through with the whole shebang?"

"Yes!"

"He'd known about it all the time?" I said, mouth agape.

"Revenge is a dish best served muffled. Ho ho ho."

The landlord began polishing the brass on the beer pumps, his laughter pinging off the optics and reverberating around the wine glasses. I looked above the optics, at some glass cases fixed to the walls and filled with stuffed animals. A taxidermist's glorious gallery. The fox and the owl and the badger. All too late for revenge.

"Muffle seen you for a while, lad," said the landlord.

"Needed to get away."

"No place like this."

"Yeah," I said, swilling my beer around and around and around, staring absently into the miniature vortex.

I chucked the rest of the pint down my throat and ordered another. Then I was gobsmacked; Helen walked in. What the hell was *she* rolling up for? Cracking escape from Back Road, this. If it had to be anybody, why not Zebedee or Jessica or Billy? I'm thinking, not Helen, she's so dull.

"Helen? What are you...?" I said.

"What are *you* doing here?" she asked.

"Shouldn't you be...?"

"Preparing lessons?" she said, eyebrows raised.

"Well, yeah."

"Don't you know about my horses, Pete?"

She was in black boots and jodhpurs, caked in mud. After exercising 'Tess' and 'Durberville' on the moorland tracks in the morning she was hungry for lunch. I felt obliged to join her. We ordered roast dinners and sat by a window just across from the bar, looking out over the wild moors. I was still having a bash at showing an interest in her horsey talk as we neared the end of the food.

"Do you know anything about dressage?" she asked.

"Do I know dressage? Do I know dressage? Do bears shi... ? No. Erm, could you pass me the horseradish please?"

"Mum and Dad took me to loads of horse trials events when I was little. I used to love dressage."

"Right," I said, my attention drifting back towards the landlord.

He was pulling a pint for one of the locals; a bloke,

knocking on a bit, who was wearing a worn tweed jacket fastened with string. He only had one tooth in his head but it stuck out, big and bold, from the middle of his top gum and kept catching on his lower lip when he spoke.

"Happen one's hoiked it and it's lollpt up," said the local.

"Ho ho ho! Muffle muffle muffle, Briggsy lad," replied the landlord.

I was thinking fuck knows how they understand each other, these two. I forced myself to turn to Helen again. She was still talking about dressage.

"The control of those horses. The posture, the discipline, the hours of painstaking practice put into every step and turn. It's pretty impressive."

"Sounds it," I said.

The landlord pulled himself half a bitter with a good head on it. He took a long sip and the froth stuck to his beard like whipped cream.

"Cheers, Briggsy," he said.

"Reet do," said Briggsy.

"Hee hee hee," laughed the landlord, looking over at me.

I watched him shake with mirth as he told Briggsy about telling me the wedding story. Briggsy just had a big grin on his face, his lone gnasher resting comfortably on his bottom lip. Of course I couldn't catch all the landlord's words, but there was one which stood out to me as bold as Briggsy's tooth, "Revenge." "Revenge." It was still ringing around inside my head when I picked up on Helen and dressage again.

"And they have to plait the horses' manes in absolute

symmetry," she said. "Brush their tails until they shine, groom their coats until they shimmer, polish the saddle and tackle, attend to each hoof with meticulous care."

"Serious?" I said.

"Really boring though," she said, crunching on a roasted parsnip.

"Oh, I wouldn't say that."

"Don't lie."

"Well."

"But have you ever been to the races?"

"Erm, no."

"Never been to the races? Where have you been all your life?"

"Quite a few places, actually," I said, swallowing a lump in my throat.

"Wow, never been to the races? Those gorgeous animals pitted against each other in a stampede for the line. Ears back, muscles toned and taut, legs in a whirl. The rumble of noise and speed down the final straight, the crowd rising, roaring 'em on, hooves pounding, shaking the soil from the ground. Pete, you haven't lived!"

I aimed my fork at a final sprout, but missed and landed sloppily in gravy and mushy mash.

"What are you doing here anyway?" she asked, confidently using a stuffing ball to mop up the remaining mess on her plate.

"Needed a break."

"Is everything all right?"

"Tell me, Helen, what do you make of Deborah Styles?" I

asked.

"She's on your mind, is she?"

"Have you noticed how closely she's working with Margaret now?"

"Yes, what's going on there?" she said, placing knife and fork neatly together on her empty plate.

"Well, do you reckon she'd be so interested if Margaret wasn't after getting the council to fund some courses, at that much higher hourly teaching rate?"

"Oh she's like that, is she?"

"You bet she's like that."

"I am uncomfortable about the way she talks to her students."

"Yeah, you see. There's another thing. It could actually be regarded as abuse, the way she speaks to them, you know."

She shot me a quizzical look.

"Abuse?" she said.

Chapter Nine

On the Tuesday afternoon following bank holiday, when the students had gone home and the flimsy partitions had been folded and stacked against the walls, the teachers were sitting in a circle at Back Road. We were awaiting Margaret. In the morning she'd announced that a meeting, compulsory for all staff, was to be held. By the time morning break was over, after whisperings behind cupped hands and utterances under fag-time umbrellas, everyone knew about Styles and Margaret on the Friday before, tucked away in the office, drawing up proposals. It had irked everybody and we were unanimous; something had to be said. And the meeting, which surely related to the matter, was our chance to show some unity.

As well as the backing of my colleagues, the long weekend in the village had helped to calm me. The remoteness, the wilderness, had offered some perspective, and Helen, over apple pie and cream, had convinced me that I could overcome any unfairness by simply stating my point of view clearly and honestly to Margaret. Now, the meeting would present us all with the opportunity to do so. We would simply inform Margaret that to draw up proposals for the council without first consulting every teacher was unacceptable. Our concerns about favouritism, and the disproportionate influence of a particular one of our number, would be voiced most resolutely etc. etc.

As I said, I *had* calmed down. At lunchtime I even sensed some bounce in my walk, as if I was at last about to realise my dream of heading up the vanguard towards fairness and morality. In fact I couldn't wait for Styles to rock up for her afternoon dance session, so I could look her in the eye and commence the fight back. Then I was having a chinwag with Helen in a room off the main hall, where us teachers have our sandwiches. I was tucking into a BLT and a bag of cheese and onion as she took her time over salad and rye bread.

"I mean, drawing up proposals without even asking us," I said. "I don't know what's happened to our Marge. Well I do, it's about four foot ten and full of shit. Sorry. Sorry, Helen."

"We should stay calm, Pete, that's all. We can be forceful about our misgivings, but only in an assertive way. As soon as we start being aggressive..."

Then the door swung open and Zebedee was standing there, as if it's a saloon and he's in a western.

"You won't believe this, dudes," he said.

"What is it, man?" I asked.

"Madam Styles will not be showing this aft."

"You what?"

"Flu type symptoms is the word on the street."

"Flu type symptoms? She's taking the bloody piss. Can't face the music-itus, more like. Can't face us, can't hack it. Gutless, that's what she is. You know that?"

"Pete, the fact remains that the best thing we can do is keep calm," said Helen, delicately using a fork to push a slice of tomato onto her rye bread.

Styles' cowardice had prevented her attendance yet, at the meeting, her presence still lived in the main hall, clutching the atmosphere like the acrid odour in the aftermath of a blaze. The big golden framed photograph, which hung on the wall behind where Margaret was due to sit, didn't help. It looked down on us, like an Oscar winner over defeated nominees. It was one of those clichéd pictures you sometimes see advertising musicals; where the star turn is placed on one knee at the front, nose to the camera lens, arms outstretched to embrace the adulation of the world. And behind the star, the chorus. Dovetailing in a glitzy, star-spangled human fan. The stereotyped image for razzmatazz. Only, this picture differed from the stereotype in that the star turn was not, in fact, the star turn. It was a fifty year old woman, squat of stature, plain of attire, whose job was supposed to be behind the lens. Madam Director herself. Was it about her? Was Back Road there for the teachers or the students? From the circle, I glanced up at the image. For a painful moment I faced the thought that, with that egotist inside me, I shared a shameful characteristic with this woman. Hadn't I wanted all the glory for myself? Wasn't that me? Then I glimpsed the light outlining her slightly opened mouth and the tongue only partially obscured. The tongue that, when she talked, betrayed itself erratically in flickers from behind uneven teeth. In most people similar mannerisms are simply quirky but, in her, this involuntary reflex appears to assume a sinister edge. But then she's known for deceit and manipulation. What does she expect?

Now the circle had quietened. Anticipation grew. At times the quiet dispersed to leave an absolute silence, only broken when someone offered an ironic platitude or a shit joke. Zebedee, dazed and distracted, plucked absently at an unplugged electric guitar. Billy slumped in his chair, scribbling kites and clouds in a dog-eared jotter. Helen sat holding her pen over a leather bound notebook, which at least made me smile because it looked like the notebook for special occasions. She meant business and the thought sort of reassured me again. But then I looked at Jessica, her face set like sculpture, staring unwaveringly at the gaudy showbiz image of Styles. This woman coming in from nowhere, seemingly trying to exploit, for financial gain, a place set up to help others. Jessica, due to personal circumstance, might have been obsessing about the money side of things but I could empathise with her anger. I was right there with her on that one. Except, for me, it was more the exploitation *per se* which I couldn't stomach. The fact that somebody had the brass bollocks to waltz into Back Road, thinking not of others but only of herself. Perhaps I was seeing too much of myself in her; my old self, before I started at Back Road. Maybe I was seeing too much of that selfish ego from which I thought I'd been escaping.

Margaret at last walked into the room, her staccato steps quick yet disjointed, like a squady late for parade. Her body did not seem to believe in the orders it had been given. She moved to her chair in this way and looked at no one. She must have felt the silence but she betrayed no acknowledgement of it. She was just trying to hold herself together. She sat in the circle, swung her feet under her chair, put her knees together, rested various papers in her lap and hunched over the documents under a pretence of perusal. She wasn't reading. She was trying to claw back some composure. We could all tell because her edginess broke rudely into the silence in short heavy breaths and her hands shook exaggeratedly. This was the woman who'd given me a shot at redemption. "You can offer so much here, Pete," she'd said. "A man of your calibre." It was like she was lending me some of her confidence, loaning out her hard fought self belief. "Look what it's like if you believe in yourself, lad," she seemed to be saying. "Look what you can do. You can achieve something which really matters." Was this that person?

Moments before she spoke I noticed the collar on her blouse, half down, half up, like a wonky 'S', a distorted arrow. Her pride was slipping and the arrow pointed upwards to a place on her shoulder, where Deborah Styles offered a consoling, glittered embrace. She raised her gaze towards a spot just above our heads and inhaled the air deeply, hinting at a considered, measured approach. Some of her words were measured, but they were interspersed with others, blurted out as if they were naked feet traversing white-hot coals.

"Thanks for coming. You're professionals and I've come to expect this, but then we all realise how critical things have been for us. I value your attendance, your commitment. I want you to know that. Oh, Deborah can't make it unfortunately. Very unwell. Right, so what are we here for? I think you've been talking, I'm not stupid, I've seen your bothered faces. I'm sorry it... I mean, I'm not stupid. I think you have a good idea, but I need to clear things up. So we can move on. Start afresh. Like when this whole project started? Do you remember that? Some of you? The way we were? The thing is, we've been betrayed. Half our funding cut off. You know all this but it still hurts me. Like a fist around my heart. It was betrayal. How could they?"

I cast my eyes around the circle at the pairs of feet shuffling uneasily, like running spikes anticipating a starter's gun. Filled with taut tension and sinew, on the edge, waiting for the proper shit to start.

"How could they?" continued Margaret. "Anyway, the council's stepped in. Saved us really. This is the wonderful news. Yes. Yes, it is wonderful. Because all of our futures are more secure now. And, most importantly, of course, undoubtedly, the future of our students. They are, after all, what matters. Just think what would happen to them if... look, I don't mean... listen, you are all valued, never let that be forgotten. I value you all. You know that, don't you? You do know that?"

I wanted to speak, but I was afraid of what might come out. My instinct was still to protect her, to comfort, to have faith in her. To repay her. And perhaps I would have spoken, if I had not sensed within me a visceral anger vying for dominance over fading loyalty. She ploughed on.

"As we all know, we're all aware of this, receiving such a heavy financial blow has placed untold pressure on Back Road. I can't explain how painful it's been for me to have to cut your wages so... so dramatically. It's been indescribably... it has been difficult."

"Yeah, we know 'difficult.' We know all about 'difficult,'" said Jessica, looking at her nails and sucking on her teeth.

"What was I supposed to do, Jessica? Sack half of you and double the class sizes? Deny half of you a job and simultaneously dilute the students' education? No. I couldn't do it. I had no choice. If you want the truth, I have tried to make as small a cut as possible. That is the truth. And even then, even then, all because of this betrayal, we have been under threat. I mean, we can barely survive. Do you understand that, Jessica? Can you see that?... Right, let's move on. We need the council's backing. That is plain. Nobody can argue against me on that."

She took some time, pretending to scan her papers, fooling no one. It looked like she was giving herself breathing space to cool down a bit. It felt like ages. I kept peeking up at Styles doing showbiz, smiling down on me, taking the piss. And my thoughts were starting to overheat, like in some chemistry experiment when they get you to blast a test tube with a Bunsen burner and all the particles start going crazy, whizzing around in a frenzy of confusion. And this stress in my head began firing my blood, propelling it through my veins, until I could feel it pulsing at my temples. I looked around the circle. Billy's kites and clouds had become darker, heavier shapes. Jessica, a toppling stone statue, leaned on him. Zebedee had stood his guitar up between his legs, to imagine it a double bass, and was now plucking away like some laid back dude in a nineteen twenties' speakeasy. Helen slid a ruler from the back of her notebook and scribed a perfect line under a subheading. We were all just treading water, awaiting news. When Margaret at last spoke again, her indignant riposte to Jessica appeared to have given her back some conviction.

"As you are aware, the council has sanctioned the funding of some of our programme. I can now confirm they are prepared to back courses aimed at promoting students' life skills. Self-advocacy, independent living, making choices. Essentially these fundamental aspects. Clearly, this is to be welcomed by us all because it encompasses a significant proportion of our work. Our mission. Thanks to the council, we can now survive. And your jobs are safe once more. Furthermore, you will all receive a boost in earnings. We have secured funding for every teacher here. Each of you will now have at least one of your courses financed by the council."

Boing! Fizzz! Zebedee had snapped a string.

"One? Is that it?" he said.

"In some cases, yes. In some cases, two. But it's a start..."

Those particles in my head had just been shot through with another blast of fire.

"Hang on, are you saying these funded courses have already been dished out? You've already discussed these proposals with the council and had them approved? You and Liza Minelli up there?" I said, pointing at the picture.

She began fingering through her papers again, bowing her head, wordlessly answering my questions.

"Would it not have been correct protocol to consult us all first?" asked Helen, fighting to maintain that air of professionalism. Margaret hesitated once more, stroking her jaw, searching for reassurance, as half stifled sighs punctuated her breath. The teachers, casting dithered glances at each other across the circle, shifted in their seats.

"We had to decide," Margaret eventually said, stumbling on. "They... they wanted clear answers. About what we, you know, what we could deliver. I couldn't risk losing this chance. This… this opportunity to save our skin."

"But you've done this over bank holiday. When we were all out of the way. You've done this behind our backs, Margaret," I said.

"It wasn't…"

"What's she got?" asked Jessica, her tone like cold steel, her stare fixed on a point above Margaret's shoulder. Billy's biro penetrated the jotter paper, plunging into a black cross. Everyone froze.

"Who?" said Margaret, as if she was just throwing another question into the conversation, like she really didn't know who was being referred to.

"What's she got?" said Jessica, stabbing her finger at the star-spangled Styles.

"Deborah? Oh, well, she. She has a lot of experience in the area of life skills and… to be honest, they were very impressed with her. And, as I said, we needed to secure our future and… her past experience, well they were willing to back it and they were not so sure about funding others and if they hadn't relieved some of the burden, our burden by financing her courses then…"

"So we're expected to be grateful to her?" I said.

She clammed up at that. The teachers were talking now, in twos and threes they faced each other, murmuring, shaking their heads. Previously pent up emotion was leaking into the room through mouths and nostrils and pores in the skin. Only Jessica was motionless and silent, her feelings locked up again tightly inside. A minute or so passed before she spoke once more, shutting up the rest of us.

"How many courses has she got out of them?" her voice was almost monotone now, as if all the soul had gone out of it.

"Who, Deborah?"said Margaret, ungraciously wiping sweat from around her lips.

"How many have they given her?"

"As I say, they were impressed with..."

"How many has she got?" said Jessica, coldly.

"Well, quite a lot because, as I say..."

"How many?"

"Ok then. I mean, you won't let it lie, will you?"

"How many?"

"You want to know? You won't let it lie! You want to know, do you?"

"Yes! I want to know!" cried Jessica, leaning towards her.

"Eight," said Margaret, her head suddenly lolling forwards, hanging limply, like it had just been knocked senseless.

Around the circle jaws dropped, gasps sucked up the thick air. Eight fucking sessions! I could have sworn there was a miniature drummer banging away at my temples.

"Have they done their checks on her?" I said.

"They do their checks on everybody," said Margaret, slowly raising her head again.

"Whilst we're on about it, have *we* done checks on her?"

"Yes we have done our checks. What kind of place...?"

But her anger was no match for mine.

"In fact, Margaret, answer me this. Should she really be working with vulnerable adults at all? Have you ever even observed one of her sessions? Eh? Nearly everything she says to her students is like a put down. How can anybody develop when they're being constantly slagged off? Everyone feels crap about themselves when someone's beating them up like that. How can you be happy and fulfilled under that kind of fire? And what does it do to people with learning disabilities, when their self esteem is already up the creek half the time? Mental health? Psychological abuse? You are aware of these issues, aren't you? Margaret?"

"How can you speak to me...?" she said, the words cracking like ice cubes dropped in water.

"Pete, enough now," said Helen.

I'd had enough. I felt like shit for having a dig at her as soon as I shut up. And then, as we all looked on, incredulity gripping our faces, paralysing our movements, Jessica finally completed her transition from giggling schoolgirl to Goddess of Hellfire. Like an automaton, she marched to the gleaming picture hanging behind Margaret, reached up, removed it and smashed it against the wall. The frame cracked, the picture crumpled. Yet still I could see Styles' laughing eyes catching me in their gaze.

Chapter Ten

A couple of weeks later, the mid May sun and rain having splashed the earth with colour, I was in a 'greasy spoon' on a Sunday morning. I was waiting for Billy and Zebedee. We were due a heavy shot of cholesterol before watching the last match of the footy season at the local pitch. It was belting it down outside. I was sitting by the window watching the water stream down the glass, my hands wrapped around a pint-sized mug of tea, my retro seventies' 'parker' hanging loosely and sodden from my shoulders. I gazed at my wobbly reflection and reflected on my recent behaviour.

Apart from work and the corner shop, this was the first time I'd been out since the meeting. I'd shut myself off in my flat, living like a stoned student, eating pot noodles, drinking cider at ninety nine pence a litre. I spent whole weekends in my bedroom. It's easy once you get into it. You need two bedside tables (upturned cardboard boxes will do) so you can spread out all the necessaries within reaching distance. Then it's simple, collect the following and wallow: a kettle, container of water, noodles, fork, tobacco, roll up papers, lighter, saucer, newspapers, books, radio, gallons of cider and something to piss in. My windowless bedroom, high up in the roof, was perfect for this kind of debauchery; no outside distractions to divert the heathen from sinful indulgence. Escapism in temptation, escapism in self pity. Wallow wallow wallow. And yet, still I couldn't shed my troubled thoughts.

By the time I'd shuffled into the greasy spoon my ego was completely wasted. Yes, I'd failed in my dream to be some big shot saviour, but now I couldn't even save humble old Back Road from exploitation. And the other thing which had started to get to me was thinking about who was being manipulated more than anyone in all this; Margaret. The only person who'd been willing to forget my failings and say: "Here's a clean slate, show us what you can do, lad." And what had I done at the meeting? Had a pop at her. Tried to show her up. What was I thinking? She was being used. She wasn't deliberately setting out to favour one person over the rest of us. She was trying to save Back Road, the students, the teachers. It was just that there was now somebody on the scene unscrupulous enough to use another's fragile state of mind for her own ends. When I first met Margaret, when I saw her helping others, changing lives, she made me think of Mandela. Her work was on a smaller scale but, fundamentally, it was the same. She inspired me, even nursed my ego for a while, made me see it was possible to be happy focussing not on personal vanity but, genuinely, on the well-being of others. What a woman to be able to do that. And now she was empty inside, confused, lost, with the only person providing solace the one whose sole interest lay in perpetuating these emotions. But how could I help? What the fuck could I do about it?

As my soaked clothes warmed in the atmosphere of teapots and fry-ups, the steam rose from them and fogged up the window. I turned my attention to the cafe's interior; a classic, no frills, no nonsense British caf. Clattering, chattering noise, bellowing chef, sizzling smells, chipped formica tables, plastic tablecloths, pick your own cutlery (and polish it with a serviette to be on the safe side), squeezable brown and red sauce bottles with dried on dribbles. A shaggy dog, living out its last days curled up by the counter, and a waitress in her forties with an outdated perm and a penchant for stroking the dog every time she walks past it to pick up an order. The kind of place environmental health officers crave, so they can snap all their horror pictures for a lifetime of presentations in one fell swoop. A place well suited to my messed up mind. There was something consoling about it.

The door opened and in walked Zebedee in a long leather trench coat and a stetson. Water dripped from his clothes. He saw me and tipped his hat. Then, trying for all he was worth to suppress his natural bounce, he walked slowly up to the counter. I was only surprised I couldn't hear spurs clinking at his heels. Surely he was about to order a bourbon or a shot o' rye.

"You got any Americano coffee, honey?" he asked the waitress.

"Americano? Where'd you stroll in from? The movies?"

"Hey, Sugar, what's the beef?"

"It's stewing steak and we don't serve it 'til lunch!"

As the waitress laughed raucously at her own wit, Zebedee tried to look cool but, in little attempts to reassure himself, kept touching his face with his fingertips. As he stood there, waiting for the laughter to stop, rainwater dripped from the hem of his trench coat to form a wet patch at his feet. The dog dragged itself from its basket and slurped at the water with its tattered tongue.

"Ruff! Ruff! Back!" cried the waitress. "What did you

say you wanted?"

"Mug of instant granulated," said Zebedee, forlornly.

"Well sit down and I'll bring it over."

Zebedee trudged over to join me and I laughed for the first time in a fortnight.

"Howdy, Sheriff."

"Sod off."

"If you can't get a decent coffee in the middle of a western, then where, pal?"

He slumped into the chair opposite me, hunching over the salt and pepper and the manky looking ketchup bottle. He picked up a serviette, self consciously tearing it into strips, looking down at his hands as they worked away slowly.

"Do they sell chocolate here?" I eventually asked.

"Dunno."

"Oh. Just wondered if they did Bounty."

"Funny bloke, aren't you?" said Zebedee.

He started shaking a bit. He wanted to laugh but his pride was fighting it, trying to lock it up.

"Come on, soft lad," I said.

Then he looked at me and we both cracked up. We were still tittering away when Billy came in. We shut up when we saw him. Jessica had been off sick since the meeting and he'd stayed with her for every possible minute. And now, standing there in the cafe, his usual dishevelled look might have been accentuated by the downpour, but it was the look in his eyes. He seemed so vacant, as if he'd forgotten how to blink.

"Billy. Billy," said Zebedee.

"Billy?" I asked, perplexed.

"Billy!" shouted Zebedee.

"Oy! Mouth!" exclaimed the waitress, as she plonked Zebedee's coffee in front of him.

"Good golly, you're beautiful," said Zebedee. "Come on, plant one there for me," pointing at his cheek. "Go on, a big fat juicy smackerooney."

"I'll plant something there. Ever see Hagler fight?"

"Who he?"

"Too young," I said. "Billy?"

"Marvellous Marvin," she said, indicating a poster above a fruit machine. "He possessed a very handy right hook." She smiled triumphantly, turned on her heels and returned to the counter to stroke the dog.

Billy was standing in the wet patch left by Zebedee's coat, looking at the specials board, seeing nothing. I went to him, put an arm across his huge shoulders and guided him to our table. For a minute or so he sat there silently, like the witness to an horrific accident. We tried to get through to him with a 'good cop good cop' routine, but he just started welling up. This disconcerted Zebedee until he wasn't sure where to look. At last he settled on his cowboy boots, as if they were a security blanket to a toddler. When Billy did speak his lips trembled.

"Looks like there's nowt more I can do for her now, lads."

"What do you mean, kid?" I asked.

"Been talking to her, been listening, bringing her what she needs, trying to reason wi' her, but she won't even get out o' bed."

"Serious?" I said.

"She's in a right mess, won't even listen to me. I've been up all night, pacing t' floor, banging me head against walls, been staring into space. I'll catch meself staring, looking at nothing. Then, for no reason, I'll snap out of it and I'll think 'how long have I been here just standing, staring?' Don't know, don't care. All I care about is Jess. No answers anymore. She's just in that bed and she looks a state, she looks such a bloody..."

He was staring again, eyes immovable, locked on the steamed up window. The waitress shouted across the room at Zebedee.

"Eh, Jessie James? Your friend ordering, is he?"

"Not yet," said Zebedee.

"Well he needs to order. He can't just come in here..."

"Not yet!" said Zebedee.

She glared at him, but the force of his tone dissuaded her from further action. She withdrew a long pronged comb from a pocket and began vigorously tending to her perm. Billy came back to us again.

"When we first got together she didn't want me to go round to hers, 'cos her kids 'd be upset their dad had been replaced. Then, one night, kids were staying at their grandma's, so I could go round. And when I were two doors away from hers I heard this: "Billy! Billy!" Like a whisper but louder. I looked up and she were up this tree, trying not to laugh. She had a fist in her mouth and she were pointing wi' her other hand. I looked where she were pointing and I saw her husband trying to get into t' house. She'd changed t' locks, see. Anyway, I dived behind a bush, he kicked t' door and stormed off. Jess started laughing her head off. Then she got me to climb up. We just stayed up there, watching folk, laughing, 'til it got dark."

He dug his thumb and forefinger into the inner corners of his eyes and his massive shoulders began shaking under the weight of emotion. I laid the palm of my hand across the back of his head.

"What's put her in such a state, Billy lad?" I said. "Is it all this scandalous work stuff that's been going on?"

"None o' this is her fault, that's what gets me. It were her husband that left her in t' first place. I didn't put me big boot in there and split 'em up, you know. And has he been paying his way, paying his maintenance for t' kids? Has he bugger. Is there any wonder she's suffering like this?"

"There's no wonder, lad. All this worry about her kids, not having enough money to properly clothe and feed them? Course there's no wonder it's taken her to the edge. But it's this work stuff that's tipped her over, eh? It's Deborah Styles who's delivered the knockout blow, right?" I said.

I was leaning forward, bending my neck, searching for his eyes. He pinched the top of his nose and released his fingers. He stared, red and raw, at me.

"It must be," he said.

I leaned back in my chair, relieved somehow. Then I remembered the waitress talking about Hagler. I'd seen him fight many times in the eighties. One of the greats; powerful, relentless, fearless. I looked around the cafe walls and there he was, pictures of his legendary fights on every surface, at every corner. Coming at me from all angles, just as it must have been for his opponents. Perhaps not quite. Those poor bastards. He beat the living shit out of most of them. His power, his determination, his speed, his bravery. It was enough to destroy just about everything put before him. Magnificent. But then there was one fight; Sugar Ray Leonard. I was back there in my imagination now, I could have been ringside. Hagler poured forward as usual, punch after punch after punch, but Sugar Ray was quick and he was smart. The great man struggled to lay anything on him. Sugar Ray dodged and swayed and Hagler kept missing and missing and Sugar started counterpunching, jabs and uppercuts, not with Hagler's power but accurate, stinging, sharp. Hagler lost. Marvellous Marvin did not look so marvellous anymore. He'd been beaten by superior tactics, intelligence, strategy.

I snapped out of these memories and levelled my gaze at Billy and Zebedee.

"We're in a proper fight here," I said.

Chapter Eleven

One summer morning soon afterwards I was walking to work along tree-lined pathways. I imagined the cherry blossom still blooming and it blurred into the heavily laden rhododendron trees I'd passed, trekking in the Nepalese Himalayas.

Now I was back there, at sunrise, standing in child-like awe before these miracles of creation. Their dangerous snow-capped beauty, decorated in heartbreaking orange sunlight, was catching my breath in the thin crisp air. And inevitably the bird of prey was there, somewhere between the mountains and me, gliding across a spectrum of perspective. From base camps to summits in seconds. The messenger. Making it look as easy as apple pie, this journey from obscurity to glory. Was it mocking me even then? Along with the Sherpas and their contented smiles, which really should have been grimaces, considering the ridiculous weights they were carrying across that daunting landscape. As I approached 14, Back Road, images of these super humans began walking around inside my head. Serenely striding along jagged crumbling Himalayan pathways on seemingly impossible journeys. Uphill all the way, towards hidden bazaars and trading posts thousands of feet up. On their backs, reaching skyward, were the huge blocks of wares which looked as if they'd been hewn from the very mountain rock itself. Stacked high and wide like monoliths to sacred Everest, the "Goddess Mother of the Land." Pilgrimage after pilgrimage after pilgrimage. Uphill all the way. And, as I walked into number 14, I experienced again just how I'd felt about the

Sherpa's when I'd stayed in their country; to me, their promised land had already been reached. These journeys *were* their destination. In body and mind they were where they wanted to be. I could see it in their smiles. Their lives had meaning and purpose, and I was as jealous as hell.

That morning I was teaching Literacy, working one to one with Anna, a 'relatively autonomous learner.' She learns best and develops more self confidence if I set her exercises and allow her to get on with it, offering prompts and guidance only when necessary. Ideally I should have been absolutely focussed on her at all times, but the nature of the session allowed me to observe what else was going on around me. And, straight up, if I'd been standing waist deep in a pit of cobras, teaching them not to bite, I'd have been distracted by what was happening at the other end of the room.

Two sessions were taking place next to each other, separated only by one of the warped, mobile partitions: Helen and Art for students with profound disabilities, and Deborah Styles and Dance for anyone who fancied a boogie. I could see Helen and Styles through the gaps left in the partitions, which acted as entrances for each session. Some of Helen's learners, wrapped up in sedentary tasks, were visible to me. Those assigned to Styles flitted in and out of sight, as they moved around their space responding to the music. In Helen's class students were variously occupied and supported according to their individual needs. Appropriate resources were provided to make learning accessible to all. Everyone had portfolios of their work in which progress was clearly recorded and, accordingly, learning aims redefined. Helen, like an eminent conductor, was perfectly judging the balance between challenging learners to push beyond their comfort zones and being sensitive to issues of insecurity and low self-esteem. Sitting there, I was watching standards the rest of us aspire to only in a world of fantasy. A woman dedicated and brilliant. Although, that morning, I could see she was a bit ruffled; her usual calmness broken here and there in frowns, when she glanced across towards the racket coming from the other side of the partition.

The Dance class was pounding along noisily to the rhythm of a nineteen eighties' hits medley, the sound of a New Romantics' revival pervading the whole room and encroaching upon every session: Spandau Ballet flicked and preened their hairdos over Computers, Adam and the Ants marched militarily around Photography and Madonna, in bra and suspenders and carrying a crucifix, walked suggestively through Fitness. Styles was standing at the edge of the session, seemingly uninterested in it. She was talking to two people, still in their teens; a lad with a meticulously clipped beard and a lass in a rainbow coloured top. I hadn't seen them before but they looked like sixth formers carrying out a survey. They were showing Styles their folders, pointing at pages and glancing at her face, as if searching for reassurance or approval. Whatever it was they were doing there, Styles was lapping it all up. I watched her body language through suspicious eyes. All her attention was focussed on the youngsters, and she was trying so hard to make sure they knew it. She looked up intently into their faces, nodding deliberately as they talked, like a philosopher listening to

Socrates and Plato. And when her flickering tongue spoke I could just see her brow knitted in concentration, as if each experienced word might make or break such callow futures. But seriousness alone could not quite strike the perfect note. If it was to foster the desired impression, and draw the kids closer to her influence, it had to be punctuated with cordiality and humour. Periodically it looked like she was cracking a 'funny one' and underlining it with her own laughter, and placing her hands on their shoulders as if to steady herself against the power of her wit. What was she up to now? I bit down hard on my lip, seeing how far I could push it without tasting blood.

"Should that one be a capital letter?" asked Anna, indicating a worksheet.

"Sorry?" I said.

"That one, there. The 'B', yeah the 'B', the 'B.' That one."

"Sorry, Anna. Right, well what's that before it?"

"Full stop."

"Yes, so..."

"Oh yeah yeah yeah yeah. New sentence. Capital letter. Yeah yeah. Capital letter."

"You've got it, girl. You've got the moves."

"Yeah yeah, I've got the moves!"

Anna continued with her worksheet and, feeling guilty for not paying attention, I watched over her for a while. But there was always that Romantics' music rattling across the room, tapping away at my eardrums. Tempting me like a sin. It wasn't long before I couldn't help but return my attention to the Dance session, with its pervasive noise, its student action passing in and out of view. By now, Tenpole Tudor were belting out their classic, 'Swords Of A Thousand Men,' and the students were all over the place. Kerry was gazing over towards the window, no doubt ogling the postman again, Stevo was touching noses with Glenys, who kept telling him to fuck off, Julian was scratching his arse and Sylvia was weaving her way through the session in her wheelchair, waving like the Queen. There was, however, one trio of students dancing in the centre of the space, straight in my eye line. They were employing the style of The Okey Cokey. "Oohrah oohrah oohrah yey," they sang, gravitating towards each other, creating a shouted crescendo as they reached the chorus climax. "Over the hill with the swords of a thousand men!" And, as the song unfolded, they grew louder and louder.

Circling the periphery of the dance area, in view, out of view, in view, out of view, looking intensely at the floor and wagging a finger in perfect time to the beat, was Tony. The beat helped him think. And what Tony thought about mostly was fire. Or, thankfully, its prevention. He is a regular visitor to the local fire station, where he's treated to health and safety demonstrations and action packed fire drills. I think he fell in love with the chief fire officer the day he first clapped eyes on him. Today he was proudly wearing his fireman's boots, some clodhopper cast offs presented to him by 'the lads' on his birthday.

I looked on, open-mouthed, as the song unfolded and the scene's intensity and volume increased. Helen, in the eye of the storm, at times grimacing like a boatswain amid lashing waves, was doing stoically just to keep her class on task. She'd begun working with Owen, a young bloke at the extremely profound end of the autistic spectrum. With a pen and paper each, they sat together. Helen slowly drew shapes and, very gradually, Owen began copying her. Then his growing confidence encouraged him to take more initiative. He started drawing his own shapes and she began copying him. It had taken them months to get to this level of interaction. And Helen was absolutely aware that, should Owen be exposed to too much stress, he was liable to lose it, down tools, overturn tables, pull his hair out in clumps. The whole shebang would clatter to the floor and have to be rebuilt from ground zero.

Tenpole Tudor were cranking it up now with repeated "oohrahoohrahoohrahyeys." Styles, still oblivious to the impact of her class on the rest of the room, continued to impress the teenagers, this time with profound looks into the middle distance. Kerry treated the postman to a wolf-whistle, Glenys changed her mind about Stevo and locked him into a tongue sandwich, Julian decided his balls were itchier than his arse. Sylvia augmented her royal wave with a repeatedly high-pitched "we are not amused," Tony's big boots began clomping and stomping in synchronicity with his wagging finger and the trio slapped a couple of 'high fives' and some American style hollering into their routine. "Oohrahoohrahhoorahyey, over the hill with the swords of a thousand men!"

This was all too much for Helen. At last, her phlegmatic resolve broke and, for once, she cast aside her professionalism. She stood up, tugged back the separating partition, strode into the dance class, headed for the stereo and pressed the stop button. The rest of the room quietened immediately, wondering at the sudden change in atmosphere. Teachers, support assistants and students stretched their necks around the edges of the partitions, looking alertly in on Styles' class. When Helen had irritably pulled back the divide between herself and Styles she'd left the dance session more exposed, so now we could see most of what was going on in there. And the room was near silent now, trying to anticipate what might happen next. We could hear every charged word. Helen faced Styles, who inclined her head slightly to one side, looking quizzically at her.

"Problem?" said Styles.

"Deborah. It is a challenge for *anyone* to focus on task here this morning."

"Focus on task?"

The mocking tone made Helen pause momentarily. Her face flushed.

"I am all for fun but..." she said.

"Are you?"

"I am all for fun. However, at times, it can prevent learning from..."

"Ever thought of lightening up a touch, Helen? Just a tad? No, honestly. Come on, we all need a laugh. Best medicine, don't they say? I am sure it's been proven. Yes, I'm certain. Don't they say children learn best when they're having fun?"

Beside me, Anna drew breath sharply and dropped her pen.

"Do you think we're teaching children here, Deborah?" asked Helen, her voice quavering but just about under control.

Styles was thrown a bit by that. Her eyes darted, left, right, up, down, searching for a response.

"Get back to your colouring in, can't you?" she eventually said.

All the'dancers' had stopped what they were doing, except Tony. His mind was still dancing to fire's tune and the rhythm of his thoughts continued to be beaten out through the soles of his boots. Stomp stomp stomp, he circled, stomp stomp stomp.

"Tony, the music's stopped," Anna exclaimed from across the room, "Tony!"

Everyone looked over towards her. So did Tony, forgetting the direction being taken by his boots, which were now too fired up to stop.

"Aaaah!" cried Styles, as one big clodhopper landed, "My foot! My bloody foot!"

"Sorry, sorry, sorry, sorry, Deborah," said Tony, backing away.

"You idiot! Stupid bloody fool!" she raged, hobbling, grimacing, "Are you so thick you can't even look where you're going? Are you really such an imbecile? You moron!"

With her weight on her good foot, she looked down at the other. It was barely touching the ground, as if it was an animal's paw with a glass shard embedded. She slowly turned her head back towards Tony, her eyes cooling, hardening like lava as it blackens.

"Unless, of course, you did it on purpose," she said, each

word clipped like a toenail.

At that, carrying my chair, I moved quickly across the room to Tony. I guided him to sit down. There he sat, in the middle of the dance area, staring at his boots.

"Everything all right, Tony?" I asked.

"It's me who needs the chair, don't you think?" said Styles. "He could have broken my foot. I may never have danced again!"

"Everything all right, Deborah?" I said, edging a little closer to her.

Silence.

"Everything *all right*, Deborah?" I said, grinding the question out.

Silence. I saw Helen staring at Styles, motionless, utterly gobsmacked. And then, through the silence, Styles smiled at us all. It was a kind of twisted smile. Like the ones you get from gangsters in movies, when they've just been socked in the teeth and they're wiping blood from their mouths with the back of a fist. She now ushered the embarrassed teenagers forward a couple of steps, until everyone looking on could see them. It seemed like a pretty blatant attempt to transfer the room's attention onto them. Styles somehow managed to wrestle some defiance from the depths of discomfort and, standing as tall as her height and limp foot would allow, she addressed the room.

"Allow me to introduce to you all, Rosie and Josh. They are here in a voluntary capacity. From university. Yes, university. And they shall be volunteering at Back Road for six months, as part of their degree. So they can gain work experience and observe the fantastic work we all do. And I have been assigned, by Margaret, to take on a supervisory role with regard to their placement here. They shall assist in my classes and I will be their supervisor. As you can see they are a tad nervous, so I trust I can reassure them that they have everyone's full and undivided support."

Absolute silence. Then Tony looked up from his boots.

"I am not an idiot. I am not a bloody fool. I know about health and safety. Lots of people don't know about health and safety. I'm going to the fire station tomorrow, at 10.30. I know the chief fire officer, you know. Gerry is his name. He makes me a cup of tea. Milk, two sugars, seven stirs, two taps on the rim. Gerry knows. We talk about fire safety. We'll talk about it tomorrow, at 10.30.We're doing fire prevention tomorrow. There's going to be a demonstration."

Chapter Twelve

That night in my flat, chain smoking roll ups, exhaling through the skylight, I tussled with my mind. But as the summer's late twilight cooled the earth and brought out the first stars across a darkening canopy, I still could not escape my fired-up thoughts. The madness reached a tipping point. I grabbed my coat, raced downstairs, cranked up the old motor and headed for the deep valley and the zigzag pathway.

I could just pick out the edges of the path, defined in shades by moonlight. I trod tentatively, reminded by an owl's hoot below of the sheer depth of the valley. Then I stood on a round stone at the path's edge. I felt it turn underfoot and heard the squelching suck as it escaped its boggy socket, like the hideous gouging of a giant eye. My legs splayed and my fingers clutched at the grassy valley side. I stayed stock still, listening to the stone fall and crash, with death's potential at my shoulder. I was back in my childhood bedroom, the danger so close, one mad moment away. Time seemed suspended. At last the owl repeated its hoot and snapped me from my reverie. I dragged myself back to a standing position and continued on along the pathway until I reached the two blocks of square rock. I sat between them, dangling my legs above the valley, like a charity fundraiser on the threshold of a maiden skydive.

As I looked up at the stars the cool air blurred my eyes and it was like I'd returned to the Outback. Gradually, the blue-black sky seemed ever more star-filled, as in the pollution free heart of Australia. I was back there, hitchhiking, kipping rough in a sleeping bag drawn around the neck to keep out deadly scorpions. Searching for meaning in that sky blew my mind. Were the stars telling me of my insignificance in the grand scheme of the universe? Were they pinpricks of enlightenment, highlighting the preciousness of all life? What was I, precious or insignificant? Was my big fat ego to be fed and nurtured or dashed on the scorched ochre earth? I knew it was Styles who'd collared me and dragged me back to these existential questions, along with all their disturbing reality. I'd escaped them for a while, been almost content in my role at Back Road, but now they'd returned, fizzing around inside my head like miniature meteors burning across the sky. Only they were back with an intensity I had not previously experienced. When I'd first contemplated them in Oz, under the inspiration of celestial beauty and infatuation, such questions seemed to mark out an opportunity. They appeared as portentous signposts at the beginning of a journey to fulfil my potential. To really do something with my life, on a big scale, with all the credit to boot. Now it felt like Styles had twisted these questions and dipped them in cynicism. The owl hooted from the depths of the valley and my heart jumped. I imagined the bird of prey's hooked beak, the tongue darting from it, and the image of Styles came to me, nagging her questions at my ear.

'Are you precious? Or are you insignificant? Come on, egotist. What are you? Are you precious or are you nothing? Did you save the world? Are you the new Mandela? Or did you end up trying to convince yourself how worthy it is to work in some shitty little backstreet charity? You class yourself as a teacher, don't you? When will you learn? Not many reach the stars. The odd lucky bastard, maybe. But the rest of us? We're of no significance. We are not precious. Wake up! We take what we can get. That is all there is. We take what we can get. You might have looked up at the stars, egotist, but I think you've finished up in the gutter with the rest of us.'

I gazed at the river flowing silently below. The moon's reflection appeared diffused and fractured across its surface as eddies and whirlpools played with the light. Then I saw the owl gliding serenely on the breeze just above the water, a dark shape set against the glinting river. I felt the breeze gently touch my cheeks, the valley air like a seductress in a Shakespearean tragedy. I looked between my dangling feet as the owl glided deep down beneath me. The breeze curled around my head, caressed my neck. I lost sight of the owl and leaned forwards, trying to recapture its silhouetted image. I wanted to follow its path, the arc of its journey above the meandering river. Like Peter Pan, I wanted to fly away off the ledge and escape into the depths of the valley. Not wanting to do it, but wanting to. The boy who never grew up. But then something caught my eye and an instinct jerked my gaze skyward. A shooting star burned a straight line across the heavens. So fast it was like a flash. And for that tiny moment there was nothing else in all of the earth and its universe. Nothing. For that one moment all else was forgotten. When it was gone I blinked and I glimpsed its brightness once more, as if I'd been looking at the sun. I shivered and then froze and then clamped my lids shut. And there it was again, burning away behind my eyes.

Chapter Thirteen

It was Helen who suggested we all meet at Jessica's. We'd both come to the conclusion that the whole situation was getting on everybody's tits and we needed to talk things through. Helen, the consummate multi-tasker, thought that if Jessica was up for it, going to hers would give us an opportunity to offer our support and bring her round a bit. Billy had managed to persuade Jessica that this was a good idea. Although, from what he said, it sounded more like she couldn't muster the energy to mount a protest.

When Helen and I arrived in the late sunny afternoon, Billy answered the door and took us through the house to the back garden. It looked like the kids had been staying at their grandparent's or their dad's for a while, because three small bikes were propped against the fence with grass growing up between the spokes. Jessica was sitting in one of those wicker chairs you suspend from trees. She was wearing one of Billy's gigantic jumpers and drinking tea with her knees tucked up under her chin. We turned quizzically to Billy, searching for a clue as to how we should approach her, but he just sighed and shrugged his big shoulders and asked us what we wanted to drink. As he moved back into the kitchen we sat on the grass near Jessica, taking a stab at a distance not too invasive. In the kind of tone I imagined she'd use to reassure a spooked filly, Helen spoke.

"Hey, Jessica. Hey, Jess."

Jessica, suspended above us, looked into our faces for a moment.

"Good of you to come," she said.

"How are you?" asked Helen.

"Tired."

I looked at Helen and there was a tacit acknowledgement between us that perhaps we should just sit quietly until Billy came back. But then we heard a loud knocking at the front door. A sort of rhythmical rap.

"Zebedee," I said.

When he boinged into the garden, it was obvious he'd been flashing his loan about again. He had a spanking new acoustic guitar strapped across his back and his trousers were shimmering, skin-tight black leather. He sat next to us on the grass.

"Nice strides, dude," I said.

"Check out the new cut," he said.

Billy soon returned with mugs of tea for everyone, except Zebedee who had his customary coffee. A brew so thick and rich it made me think of those old Bisto adverts with the smell floating down streets to coax back kids for their dinners. But, judging by Jessica's depressed demeanour, there were no kids coming back today. Her chair swung almost imperceptibly from the bough, which we could hear quietly creaking during the silent breaks in our conversation. At first we limited ourselves to small talk and awkward mockery of Zebedee in lustrous leather, but we all knew what we'd really come to talk about. The difficulty was that Jessica didn't look ready for it. The idea of meeting here was beginning to look like a mistake. At last, Billy intervened.

"Listen folks, great to see you, but happen another day,

eh?"

"I can make my own decisions, Billy," came back Jessica, out of nowhere.

That took us all aback. Billy looked up at her with wide moistening eyes. She touched his cheek.

"You're a wonderful man, Billy," she said.

I think we were all welling up at that.

"What's the latest, then?" she asked.

"You go," I said to Helen.

"Well, we are becoming increasingly worried about Deborah Styles. And, quite apart from her using her influence over Margaret to... are you all right with this, Jess?"

"Carry on. Can't spend the rest of my life swinging from this tree."

"That's true, Jess. That's true."

The bough creaked. After a pause, Helen continued.

"Right, our main focus should be on the well-being of the students at all times. That is always paramount..."

"Dead right," I said.

"They are vulnerable and, no matter how much we strive to empower them to be more independent, they will always be vulnerable..."

"And so open to neglect, exploitation."

"Yes. And we've been concerned recently about the way Deborah is acting towards her students."

"Deeply concerned."

"As Pete says, deeply concerned. There appears to be no catering for individual needs in her sessions. Students' sensitivities are apparently being ignored, most obviously in the way Deborah talks to her learners. We've noticed she can be overly critical, which is very damaging for our students in particular, and that she tends to treat them like children."

"And every single time she does that, it's a kick in the teeth for their self-esteem."

"Yes, Pete. Thanks. But what has struck us most of all is the incident which happened a few days ago, involving Deborah and Tony. Zeb and Billy weren't there but we've told them about it, Jess. Have you heard?"

Jessica, shaking her head, sat up straighter in the wicker chair. And now I couldn't resist taking up the crusade.

"Tony accidently stands on her foot and she's piling into him like he's committed murder, isn't she, Helen? She's bawling at him. Calling him an idiot, thick, a fool. A moron! Seething, she was. I thought there was a lot of hatred in that voice, actually. She even starts accusing the poor bloke of doing it on purpose. And she's worried he might have broken her foot, ruined her 'dance career.' Like that'd be a terrible loss for the world. What dance career, anyway? I tell you, I wouldn't blame him if he had done it on purpose."

They were all staring at me.

"Well. Okay. Sorry, but do you reckon she gave a toss about Tony's feelings? How he felt, being called all those things in front of everyone?"

"Is she really as bad as that though, man?" Zebedee chipped in.

"I don't believe you. Were you there?" I said.

"Maybe it felt like her foot was crushed in or something," said Zebedee. "Maybe she just got all messed up. Is she really like that? That's all I'm saying."

"Have you not been listening to Helen? Have you not seen what Styles is like for yourself? I mean, take that session when Tony stood on her foot, if you want. Before the incident, we're left battling away through our own sessions because there *she* is banging out a load of eighties stuff at full blast, isn't she Helen? Not a thought for anyone else in that room except herself, had she? At least when you're doing sessions, Zeb, you tone it down a bit. It's not even that though. There's no teaching going on, she didn't even cast her students a glance, did she Helen? Until Tony steps in, of course. Are these the marks of a professional teacher? I tell you, she's a bloody fraud. Where did she come from anyway? Does anybody know anything about her background? Who the fuck is she? And now there's these two stripling undergraduate volunteers hanging around with her. 'I am going to be their supervisor,' she says. You know, properly arrogant. Like, you know, 'Think what you want of me, but I am to be their supervisor.' What's the story there? Probably getting a backhander or something."

"How's she landed that gig, anyway?" asked Zebedee.

"Oh she'll be telling Margaret she's just sailed through a D.Phil in Supervisory Techniques, or some other bollocks. I tell you, she's in absolute control of her. She's been playing with her emotions right from the start. Margaret's as vulnerable as the students these days. Insecure, weak, paranoid even. And there's Styles, entering stage left, playing her as easily as Clapton strumming a guitar."

"Old Slow Hand," said Zebedee.

"Who does she think she is? She comes in from nowhere, accumulates all this power and starts lording it over everyone. I reckon she's obsessive, you know. Wringing out every last drop of influence over Margaret, the students, the council, us. I'm telling you, the woman's an egomaniac!"

The bough creaked. Everybody fixed their eyes on me. Zebedee plucked a line from 'Cocaine.'

"What are we going to do about it, then?" said Jessica.

"Firstly," said Helen, "we must remember that we have a duty to support and, if necessary, protect our learners in every possible way. We mustn't forget that this is about *them* and their well-being."

"I agree," I said.

"We think we need to gather more evidence about Deborah Styles' treatment of her students. We'll record what we've already witnessed, but we know more is needed if we're to take this to the council."

"Shouldn't we be teking evidence to Margaret first?" asked Billy.

"We've thought about that, Billy," I said. "And, the thing is, she's put her absolute trust in Styles. We doubt she could hack it if that trust was broken. She's too fragile."

"Suppose we've got to protect Margaret in all this as well," said Zebedee.

"Yes we do," said Helen. "Pete's right when he says she's as vulnerable as anyone. Now, the council has a whistle-blowing procedure for anyone who has concerns about the inappropriate actions of a colleague. We've looked into this and, if Deborah continues in the same vein, and we can evidence everything thoroughly and accurately, we think there might be a chance to... to have her removed from a situation in which she can neglect or harm others."

"Get her sacked, in other words," I said.

"Everything we do has to be professional and absolutely water-tight though, Pete."

"Oh yeah, I know that," I said, pulling up tufts of grass, as if they were my real preoccupation.

Before we started on the wine, we all agreed to keep our noses to the ground. Even Jessica said she thought it might do her good to keep an eye out, whenever she felt ready to come back of course. Then she asked us to stay for a 'take out' and sent me to the offy for a three litre box of red. We stopped short of raising our glasses, musketeer style, to our new mission but we christened it 'The Project.' To me it was like the first counterpunch I'd thrown. Sugar Ray! And that cheap plonk tasted like it had been bottled in a French vineyard in nineteen sixty two.

Billy split some logs and fired up a chimenia and we stayed late, gathered around the glow. There was warm conversation and Zebedee struck up some tunes. He might act like a prick, and look like a prick, half the time but sometimes you just can't help loving the stupid bastard. He wanted to entertain us that night because he craves the attention, but he also wanted to cheer us up. He always wants to cheer people up. Two minutes into his 'set' and we were all pissing ourselves. We had 'All Shook Up' with pelvic thrusts, 'Morning Glory' with a Mancunian strut and 'I Can't Get No Satisfaction' with pelvic thrusts. It was only when he was doing 'The Walk Of Life,' and trying to get us all to 'do the walk,' that he realised just how much of a prick he looked. He sat back down on the grass, sipped his wine and waited for the laughter to subside. When he'd drained his glass, he regained a bit of composure and turned to Helen.

"Right, Hell's Angel, this one's for you. Ride hard, be free. Musta-ang Sally!"

Helen looked embarrassed but the light was fading and I couldn't see properly. I know she's more comfortable giving other people attention, but I couldn't quite work it out. I think she was embarrassed, though I think she enjoyed it too. Then Zebedee changed the mood and slowed things down a bit. He looked across at Jessica, now on the grass, enveloped in Billy's arms, and sung her a Slow Hand classic; 'Wonderful Tonight.' And it was wonderful. I hate that song, but it was fucking marvellous. He sung it like he was properly grown up, and he sung it like it came from us all. And it did. I can't help it, I love that guy. He had Billy blubbing like a big baby.

Chapter Fourteen

By the time all the new council funded and Back Road funded courses started in early September, we knew exactly which ones Styles had landed from the council, along with times, dates, venues, student names, student numbers, the whole shebang. Helen had meticulously logged every piece of information in The Project Portfolio. And she'd probably locked the portfolio in a safe embedded behind a picture in her bedroom wall. Then locked the safe's combination in another safe, to which only she knew the combination.

Styles had decided not to accept any Back Road funded courses, instead just sticking with the more lucrative eight from the council. 14, Back Road would be used as a venue for some of these but most would take place 'out in the community.' We knew the council weren't keen on chaotic number 14 as a venue for learning, but it did seem mighty convenient for Styles to be away, most of the time, from the place where we could keep an eye on her. Still, the week before start of term, during a Project meeting at Helen's place, we began to see this as an opportunity. If Styles thought she was away from prying eyes, surely she would be less reticent about showing her true hand. Our first big challenge became clear; how to get close enough to these sessions out in the community. Close enough to observe and record, without being discovered.

We cracked up when Helen said it: "Disguises." Pantomime season was three months early. But then she dragged a big trunk out of her walk-in resources cupboard and gave Zebedee the once over. Dolled him all up like a pretty maid in a period drama. Admittedly, he looked a twat, and as conspicuous as consumption, but you would have had to get up close before you realised it was him. We took the point. Helen's artistic skill, applied with a bit more subtlety, could pass us off as ordinary folk, out and about, minding our own. Just as long as we didn't get too close.

"We'll have to be bloody careful, mind," said Billy, still pawing away tears of laughter brought on by the appearance of Lady Zebedee.

"Don't worry, Billy, we will be," I said, trying on hats and coats.

"Jess keeps going on about she might want to help out, see. If she fancies a go at this disguise thing. Well, she'd better not get caught. That's all I'm saying. Just as she's pulling her sen round. That's all I'm saying, Pete."

"We understand, Billy lad."

"What would happen if we did get caught?" asked Zebedee.

"We'd submit what we've observed up to that point, express our concerns about Deborah. The whistle blowing facility is there for a reason, Zeb," said Helen, wiping away his rouge, picking off his false lashes.

"Stop stressing, boys," I said. "We're not doing anything wrong. The whistle-blower procedure is in place for exactly this sort of situation. For helping to deal with someone like Styles. It's not us neglecting anyone, is it? We're doing all this in our own time, off our own bat. She's the one guilty of neglect, not us."

Billy ran a sparkly feather boa through his fat sausage fingers.

"Was it bang out of order then, the way she spoke to Tony?"

"Come off it, big man, are you serious?" I said, peering out at him from under the brim of a bowler hat.

There wasn't enough money in the Back Road kitty to fund our teaching morning and afternoon, five days a week, so we all had time off which coincided with some of Styles'sessions. I was given the first assignment. 'Exploring Leisure' was on a Tuesday morning and we'd heard the students chatting about an outing to the local public gardens. I go there all the time, to think and think some more, so I knew the place's geography. I reckoned they were destined to visit the tearooms by the model boat pool at some point; the only feature of the gardens where you can develop life skills whilst simultaneously eating cake and ice cream. Knowing how passionate some of the students are about cake and ice cream, and knowing how Styles could look upon even a vanilla slice as a vehicle of control, it seemed nailed on to me.

After breakfast on that Tuesday morning I went round to Helen's for a makeover. I have one big advantage when it comes to effective disguises. A skilfully placed wig results in a transformation because, these days, I'm as bald as an egg. She put the thing on and straightened it by pulling on the bits by my temples. Then she produced a tache from a tin and stuck it on so that only my bottom lip showed. Old National Health style glasses, with false lenses, completed the look. She stood behind me, got me to close my eyes, gently put her hands on my shoulders and pushed me towards a mirror. "Open them!" she said. We cracked up. But I couldn't even recognise myself, and you saw someone in town every two minutes who looked more out of place than the dude staring back at me. Helen had been out to buy The Guardian, which she now slipped under my arm, and I was off. Absolutely kakking it.

Walking through town I got a couple of looks, but then I realised I'd been glaring into faces to gauge reaction. I concluded that, if I didn't act like a freak, I stood a decent chance of going unnoticed. I reached Spa Gardens and made my way up the path towards the tearooms. The gardens are like the crown jewels in our town. Fountains cascade and sparkle, carefully manicured flowerbeds give off perfumed aromas which always draw in elderly tourists who say things like: 'Ooh there's some pride been put into these blooms.' But my favourite bit comes after these gaudy scented squares. The part where the trees are ancient and knarled, like old war veterans, and the tree roots snake into stagnant looking pools, and weird spiky plants squat in the shade, and the smells are earthy and dank. A rainforest in microcosm. It always reminds me of the rainforests I visited in Indonesia. But then, that morning, I had to focus on my assignment. I wanted to kick things off well for the Project. I was like a private detective on his first stakeout, desperate to report back to the aggrieved party with something concrete to go on. I took up position on a bench within earshot of the tearoom's outside tables, with their shiny laminated menus. From here I could look straight back down the path I'd just walked up, in the hope that Styles would choose the same route. I pretended to read the paper and waited.

The Exploring Leisure class began meandering up the path just as I'd turned to 'obituaries.' The moment I saw Styles I again sensed those frenzied particles in my head. I felt my face redden. My reactions were becoming instinctive, like a feral animal threatened or trapped. She'd managed to enrol most of the students from her previous dance course. Stevo, Glenys, Julian, Kerry, Sylvia. And Tony, now minus clodhoppers. The undergraduates were there; Rosie in purple and Josh with a goatee. Rosie was pushing Sylvia in her wheelchair. Josh was gesticulating, expressing something heartfelt to Styles, who walked next to her supervisees, looking up at Josh, nodding most understandingly.

At first the group was too far away for me to catch snatches of conversation on the breeze, so I could only tap into body language. Tony's deportment had a look of intense concentration about it; there was an air of purpose to his walk, yet he never seemed very far ahead of the others, only slightly peripheral to them. An authentic stranger, looking on, would have struggled to conclude whether he was a member of the party or not. Stevo, Glenys, Julian and Kerry kept stopping to touch or smell the flowers, periodically calling each other over to sample a texture or a fragrance. Sylvia pushed down determinedly on her wheels, dragging Rosie along, whenever she wanted to share in the pleasure of her friends' experience. It was beautiful to watch, because these students had previously described nature's smells and textures in my Creative Writing sessions, and drawn and pressed flowers in

Helen's Art class. Here they were showing an appreciation of what they'd learnt at Back Road. Changing lives on some miniature scale was at least better than shovelling shit around a factory.

"Sylvia, stop dragging Rosie around!"

I heard *that* from Styles. My shoulders stiffened. I lifted the paper to partially obscure my moustachioed face. Manifest in shaking broadsheet pages, my jittery nerves increased with every step of the group's approach, the nearing threat of being exposed. I tried to focus on obituaries again, not daring to look up. I imagined Stevo seeing right through me and charging over, shouting: "Eh up, Peto. What you doing here, Pal? Eh, pal, like the wig, pal! How much?" I kept my head down and soon shuddered at the clatter of metal chairs across stone, as they decided to enjoy the late summer sun. They'd chosen the tables nearest to me. I was bricking it, but I could hear every word.

"Now who would like some lovely cake?" asked Styles.

"Do they do chocolate éclairs?" said Glenys.

"Well look at the board, dear. Ye-es, the board. That's right. Go-od. Now can you see a picture of an éclair anywhere? Well, you're nodding, that's go-od."

It felt like her words were creeping slowly across my back, utterly patronising, sickly sweet.

"I fancy a donut," said Stevo.

"And have you brought sufficient funds, Steven?"

"Eh?"

"Have you got money? You know, to pay for it?"

"Yeah, course I have. What you on about? Course I have."

"All right then, fine and dandy. So, Glenys and Steven, why don't we ask Rosie to order for you, when the lady comes? Mmmm? Would that be nice?"

"I'll order me own. What's up wi' yer?" said Stevo.

"Rosie, if you wouldn't mind..."

"I can support you both, anyway," said Rosie.

"Right, Julian, Sylvia, Kerry. Would you like some lovely cake?"

"Can I have carrot cake please, Deborah?" said Julian.

"Shall we ask Josh to help you? Mmmm?"

"With chocolate sauce on top and raspberry jelly and banana truffles and green blancmange and potato pudd."

"Potato pudd? Potato pudd?" said Styles, laughing raucously.

"I'll help you, mate," said Josh.

"Sorry for laughing, Julian. It's just, potato pudd is funny, don't you think? Julian?"

"It's nice," said Julian.

Sylvia and Kerry plumped for ice cream. Then Styles turned to Tony. I had to look.

"We're a tad quiet, Tony. Are we not joining in today? What's the matter?" she was pushing her bottom lip out, like he was a three year old or something. "Are we thinking about fire engines again, Tony? We wouldn't want to miss out on the lovely cake, would we? Look, the lovely lady's here now."

"I'm not hungry today, thank you," said Tony.

"Oh deary me."

"A cup of tea, please. Milk, two sugars, seven stirs, two

taps on the rim."

"Aww, just like Gerry does for you down the station?"

"Gerry knows."

"He'll have a cuppa, love," said Styles to the waitress.

When the orders arrived, everyone got stuck in. With minds preoccupied, I could keep my paper lowered. Tony was sitting by himself, lining up his cup and saucer, teapot, little milk jug, sugar sachets, teaspoon, serviette, in millimetre perfect order. If he'd had a wig on like me, he could have passed himself off as Thora Hird in an Alan Bennett play. It didn't make me smile though, watching him. He looked so lonely.

Styles piped up again. I looked down at my paper. She was talking to the undergraduates.

"I don't wish to encroach on your studies too much, because you are both clearly extremely capable and intelligent. And I've always believed the most effective way to learn is to take on the responsibility of learning for yourself. The more you do this, the more you will learn. If you can hold onto your own thirst for learning, and it's obvious to me that desire burns brightly within you both, then you can aim for the stars. No, don't be embarrassed, I'm speaking the truth. I believe in you."

"Thanks, Deborah," said Rosie.

"Yeah cheers, Deborah," said Josh.

"I mean it, guys. You have all the talent in the world. And, having spoken to Mrs Lee at the university, I know she rates you both very highly."

"Did she say that?" asked Rosie.

"Absolutely. And I had to agree with her every single word."

She continued to lay it on thick until everyone had scoffed up. I wanted to rip off my tache and wig, storm over, overturn tables like Jesus in the marketplace. It was all so false. But I did as Helen had told me. I tried to be professional and held my nerve until they'd gone. Then I sat at one of the tearoom's outside tables, ordered coffee and made sketchy notes about what I'd witnessed.

I knew I should have kept a clearer head, recorded accurately everything I'd heard, remained objective. But objective? After the way she'd spoken to the students? They weren't babies. They were adults with learning disabilities. They had attributes, moods, idiosyncracies, problems, weaknesses, strengths, senses of humour, stupidity. Just like everybody else. Different, like everybody else. What they were not was children. What was it about Styles? What motivated her? I knew she was a greedy bastard, but there was something more than that. More fundamental perhaps. Her greed wasn't in any way sated by being so fucking patronising towards the students. The council weren't paying her any more to be such a bastard. Yet it looked like she wanted to subjugate the students all the time. Keep them absolutely under her control. If I'd been her counsellor, I'd have been tempted to take her back to her childhood, to try to get to the bottom of it. I wasn't in the mood for placatory listening techniques right now though. This was psychological abuse. But how could we prove that? "Oh well, she asked the students if they wanted some lovely cake. No, it was the way she said it. It was really patronising." It was just not going to stick. It wasn't concrete enough. I was properly pissed off now. We needed something solid, something tangible. I wouldn't have said it to Helen, but something 'sackable.' That drummer was back, whacking away at my temples. She was getting away with this. Her job was not to mock and undermine. It was to support, nurture, encourage.

I lit a roll up, ordered another coffee. And what was it with Josh and Rosie? What were they to Styles? Why was she buttering them up good and proper? Did the council know they were helping out in sessions? How much did Margaret know? We had to untangle something from all this.

Chapter Fifteen

That weekend, at another Project meeting, I reported back to Helen and Zebedee. I tried persuading them how serious Styles' treatment of the students was. I'm not sure Zebedee bought it. And I was still hacked off that we needed so much more to nail her.

"After one assignment, Pete?" said Helen. "The Project's barely started. We have to persevere, that's all."

We were discussing the undergraduates when Jessica rolled up with Billy. During the week she'd returned to Back Road to run a couple of sessions. Helen had been there and she said that she'd seemed serious and focussed on teaching. We hadn't expected her at the meeting and we weren't sure how she'd handled being back at work. We just dished out the hugs to her and the big man, filled her in on the latest and gave her some space. But then, with an edge of excitement to her voice, she said she had some useful information. She'd heard Kerry talking to Glenys about Styles' Country Life course. The group were to meet in Spa Gardens on Thursday morning, where they would walk through the rainforest bit and into the woods beyond. Zebedee and I had Thursday mornings off. The Project's second assignment was established.

Helen said, if we scanned the charity shops for khaki jackets, brown trousers, walking boots and binoculars, she'd provide the floppy hats and bushy beards and do us a fry up for Thursday breakfast. So we bowled up at hers on Thursday as birdwatchers in second-hand gear. As we tucked in at her table, she gave us a floppy hat fashion show, peppered with catwalk turns and coquettish glances. She was making us titter, trying to relax us before our assignment. And she was lightening up a bit. She was starting to thrive at the vanguard of the Project. It was like it was what she'd been searching for.

We chose our hats, Helen slapped thick beards on our mugs and two 'ornithologists' headed for the woods. I felt like Bill Oddie, but I think Zebedee thought he was in 'The Deer Hunter.' We walked through Spa Gardens, past the rainforest microcosm and into the woods. Though clear now, it had rained heavily the day before and the muddy trails amongst the trees squelched underfoot. Zebedee got down on his haunches, dipped his fingers in the mud and daubed a bit on his cheekbones. I told him we weren't supposed to be in the T.A., or the O.T.T., and poured him a coffee (decaf) from a flask. Just off the main path, we sat on tree stumps.

I was thinking about the Indonesian rainforest, where my guide told me about the virtue of looking low down and high up: 'Our lives are spent looking straight ahead or straight behind,' he had said. 'We live at one level, we miss the most beautiful, the most inspiring details.' I snapped back to today and looked up at some pine trees, their bark cracked like dried elephant skin, their needle branches curving upwards like prehistoric eyelashes. Surrounding the pine area the earth was saturated, overwhelmed by the burden of raindrops seeping from myriad ferns. The sharp smell of pine was blunted by the smell of this drenched green foliage blanketing the ground. A lone magpie cut the damp air with its rattled call.

"Plenty of cover and camouflage here, chief," said Zebedee.

"Yeah, but stop bouncing around so much. You're not Tigger in hundred acre wood. We're birdwatchers, remember. Quiet and peaceful observers."

"Received and understood, chief."

As we drained our plastic cups, Kerry, Glenys, Stevo, Julian and Tony, in bright kagools and fleeces, walked towards us along the main path. Following behind, flanked by Rosie and Josh, was Styles. She kept spreading her arms wide, like an angler exaggerating a catch, and crying out directions to the students as if herding sheep. Stealthily, we moved a little further back from the path and obscured ourselves from view behind tall trees and dense foliage. The wood's abundant plant life was so thick that, when the party passed us, we were able to follow unnoticed at a short distance, our confidence increased by disguise. The students, fascinated by nature's textures and smells, ambled slowly and stopped regularly, making it easier for us to stay still and listen. First we caught a chunk of Styles talking with the undergraduate volunteers.

"Yeah, but the deadline's in three weeks," said Josh.

"Oh come off it, Josh," said Styles.

"I'm never gonna crack this case study in three weeks."

"Just stop there, Josh," said Styles, stopping her strides, as if by way of emphasis. "Hold it right there, mate."

"I haven't even started writing it up yet and my notes are shit and... "

"Ok, time out, time out. Take five. We're going to

approach this differently from now on. From this moment, everything is going to be fine and dandy. Ok? Josh?"

"Yeah," said Josh.

"Now, this is what we'll do. We're at the church tomorrow, aren't we, guys? Could you bring your case study notes in for me?"

"Yeah."

"Good," said Styles. "Now, Rosie sweetheart, would you mind looking after this lot in drama tomorrow? Whilst I help Josh with his case study planning?"

"Well, I..." began Rosie.

"I'll set up some exercises for you, go through an example or two. We'll only be in that room on the top floor. It's very quiet, Josh. We can hear ourselves think up there, away from these noisy monsters. You know, Rosie, the room up in the loft space?"

"But will you hear me all the way up there, if anything goes wrong?"

"What's going to go wrong, Rosie? You're doing drama, not mountaineering."

"I'm only thinking about if, say, Glenys starts stressing out. You know, biting her hand and everything..."

"But I thought you had my mobile number in your phone."

"Well, I suppose, if you..."

"I think our friend just needs our support at the moment, don't you?"

"Yes... Yes, he does."

"Good. Thank you so much, Rosie."

Through the branches, as she thanked her, I caught a

glimpse of Styles holding Rosie's hand in both of hers, as if that meant twice the gratitude, twice the sincerity. Styles whistled at her flock of students and the trio began walking again to catch up.

"What's she whistling at 'em for?" said Zebedee, taking a notepad and pen from a khaki pocket.

"Make a note of it. Note everything," I said. "And underline that bit about her getting Rosie to run her session for her, so she can supervise Josh. Styles is getting paid for teaching drama to our students. I'm telling you, she'll still be claiming for it. And Rosie doesn't have the experience to be left in charge of a group of vulnerable adults. The council will be very interested in this, lad. And she'll be claiming for it, she'll be claiming all right."

"Why doesn't she just tell him she has to teach her students?"

"Note that under questions to be answered," I said. "Come on, let's catch 'em up. Get a shift on. Quietly."

We moved through the dense woods instinctively crouching but ready, if spotted, to stop and stand upright, take notes on the birdlife, look through binoculars at treetops. The ferns soaked our trousers, pine needles pricked through our clothes, branches flicked at our faces. A rush of nature blurred with adrenalin and pumped up blood pressure. Presently, the Country Life group stopped at a clearing and sat at some picnic tables in the shade of the trees. We trod carefully between fallen branches and slippery weeds, got to within five metres and crouched down low behind foliage. The breathing in my throat and the beating of my heart seemed locked in combat, fighting to be the force to give us away, battling to blast the whole project to smithereens.

"I like it when we have the grass cut in our garden," said Kerry.

"I like that. I think the grass smells *fresh* when it's cut," said Glenys.

"Yes, I do. It does smell *fresh*. Does it remind you of anything?"

"It reminds me of... it reminds me of... summer, yes summer, it reminds me of."

A long pause.

"It reminds me of my Dad, cutting the grass. When I was little," said Kerry.

"Your Dad's dead, isn't he?" asked Glenys.

"He is now. But I was a child then. When I was a child, he wasn't dead."

"He was alive?"

"Yes. But that was when I was a child. I'm an adult now. He's dead now."

"I like the smell of petrol," said Stevo.

"It's not *fresh* though," said Glenys.

"It sends me a bit loopy," said Stevo.

And peals of laughter rang around the clearing.

"Sssshhhh!" spat Styles.

Immediate and absolute silence.

"Now, I am talking to Josh and Rosie about something very important here. So, all just sit nicely please. Thank you. You have been prattling on about smelling things and touching things, so may I suggest listening for a change?

Here we are, surrounded by nature, and you are failing to appreciate it properly. Now, sit quietly and open your ears to the beautiful sounds of country life. Dear oh dear."

"Bastard!" I whispered, slightly too loudly.

"What?" said Styles, jerking her head in my direction.

A magpie's rattled call broke a new silence.

"Ok, ears open, mouths shut! Do you hear me?" she said, before turning back sweetly to Rosie and Josh. "You see guys, in my experience, whenever the stress of a situation seems too much to bear, it's up to us to gain some perspective. That is our responsibility. Throughout my career, in a wide variety of fields, I have never lost sight of this. I couldn't afford to. And that is what you must do now, Josh. I will give you the benefit of all my experience, I will always strive to do that for you, but in the end it's up to you. And you can do it, Josh. I know you can."

"You know, Deborah, I've never met anyone like you. The way you can lift somebody's spirits. I've been despairing recently."

"Oh come on, Josh, you've hardly been in despair. Tell him, Rosie."

"That's how it's felt," said Josh. "Now I feel... I feel... Deborah, you are one cool lady."

I'd moved crablike on my haunches and put my eye to a little gap between the leaves. I could see Styles' mouth trying to maintain seriousness and modesty, but flickering upwards at the corners in a subtle show of self-congratulation.

"What a lovely thing to say, Josh. Thank you," she said. "And, Rosie, please don't forget that I'm here for you as well.

Anything I can do. I mean it."

Again, she gently grasped one of Rosie's hands in both of hers, as she secured heartfelt eye contact and subdued her flickering mouth into a portrayal of empathy and altruism. Then she sort of half stood up, as if about to move towards her proper students, and this time I saw her tongue flicker. And I imagined it a flicker not erratic, but calculated. She stroked her forehead, like Columbo about to exit a suspect's room, and said, "Oh, there's something I've been meaning to ask you."

"What is it?" asked Rosie.

"Next Tuesday, Exploring Leisure, I might be a bit late. I feel bad about this but... no, I'll... No, forget it. Sorry to encroach. You've enough on your plates. What with case studies and the like..."

"Deborah, we want to help," said Josh.

"It's just, I'm supposed to be meeting Mrs Lee at the university, that's all. You know, to discuss your progress? Excellent progress, I might add. No, listen, I'll rearrange."

"How late do you think you'll be?" asked Rosie.

"An hour, top side. I booked in with her as early as possible, but I think it's too tight to catch the train I need to get over here... No, it's not fair..."

"An hour's not long though, is it? We can cope. We're all grown up now, you know. Not kids anymore," said Josh, beaming, totally chuffed to be returning a favour.

"And we know the guys pretty well now. I think we can manage, Deborah. What are you always telling us about taking on responsibility?" said Rosie.

"We'll go for coffee and cake at the station cafe and wait for your train," said Josh.

"You know something?" said Styles. "You two darlings must have been sent to me from heaven."

Using rudimentary sign language, I told Zebedee to note that Styles planned on being late next Tuesday. I was starting to reckon that everything she did was planned and calculated. My imagination had her poring over thick tomes of categorised ploys and stratagems late at night, in a room devoid of warmth, where icicles hung from a mantelpiece and pointed spikily at an empty fire grate. She controlled everything, she did everything for a reason. To her, kindnesses were a form of investment, planted seeds to be nurtured and cultivated, harvested from fields of guilt or obligation or gratitude. Josh and Rosie should have been bricking it, but Styles had actually made them feel grateful for the opportunity to help her out. I would have thought it fascinating to observe, like a birdwatcher stumbling across a cuckoo dropping its eggs into another bird's nest, if I hadn't been so incensed by her trickery. Hagler would have been baffled by such an opponent, Sugar Ray Leonard would have looked on admiringly. She was a control freak with an ego as big as mine. But here I sensed a dangerous symbiosis going on; her ego was only sustained by her being in absolute control, and this need for control was simultaneously being fired by her ego. Each element provided the other with the oxygen to breathe and flourish. Should one of the elements begin to falter? Should something be threatened or undermined? I couldn't contemplate it.

Zebedee tapped my shoulder and pointed at the ground just in front of us. There, stamped on the undergrowth, were two chunky walking boots. Tony was standing within reaching distance and looking up at a tree, tugging gently on one of the branches. Then, to get a better grip, he took a step closer. I was thinking 'fuck, if he swings on that branch, and it snaps, he's gonna land on top of me. There'll be Stevo asking how much for a false beard and Styles plotting how to get us done for harassment.' That would have put the kybosh on the whole shebang. We stayed dead still, paralysed, until Tony satisfied himself that the branch was safe and not about to fall on any unsuspecting naturalists. We knew he was off on one of his health and safety checks. He was always doing it. He set off around the periphery of the clearing, squelching his big boots into the earth, methodically testing the branches. I was waiting for Styles to notice, but she was still intent on buttering up, securing her advantage with the undergraduates. Tony was about halfway around the clearing when she caught him in her vision.

"Tony, what are you doing?" she asked, very deliberately.

"I am checking the trees for reasons of health and safety," said Tony, still intent on his task.

"Ri – ight. And could you tell us why we are all in such terrible danger from the dreaded trees?"

"There was a storm last night. The rain and the wind kept me awake. I was thinking about the trees. Hundreds of people are killed every year by falling trees and falling branches caused by storm damage. I googled that. Last night in my bedroom. When the storm was outside," he said, carefully pulling on another branch and looking at it from different angles.

"And tell us, Tony, when you googled that, was the result for fatalities worldwide, or just for this particular clearing in which we now find ourselves?"

"It can happen anywhere. Anywhere in the world."

"Did it say that, Tony? Did it really say that?"

"Anywhere where there are storms and trees."

"I think that's a bit of a useless statistic though, for our circumstances."

"It's a fact. I googled it. Last night."

"It was useless to do that though, Tony. It's an irrelevant statistic for us."

"Hundreds of people, it kills. Storm damage to trees."

"Now, if you had googled fatalities caused by falling branches in these particular woods, or even in this local area, that might have been useful. But what you've done, Tony, is completely useless."

I could see him through the foliage and, at the word 'useless,' he stopped dead still, as if he'd suddenly found himself facing a wasps' nest. There was a long pause, before he escaped back into his health and safety routine.

"Every year, hundreds of people are killed by falling trees and falling branches caused by storm damage," he said.

I soon heard the call of the magpie again and saw it hopping amongst the ferns. Then it flew up into a nearby treetop, a blur of beating wings. The blur transferred itself to my eyes, transporting me back to the Indonesian rainforest. I stared up at the magpie and it seemed half-tropical, half-exotic. Its call merged with the maddening shrieks of the rainforest and my memory jolted, the memory of my glory seeking dreams. I was consumed by them again, wanting to change thousands of lives on a really big scale, something lauded nationwide, worldwide. My mind swirled with these empty thoughts, my eyes were transfixed by the exotic magpie and Styles appeared once more inside my head, nagging her questions at my ear.

'Egotist? Listen. Sorry to encroach, but are your dreams coming true yet? Have you carried out those promises you made to yourself *all those years ago*? I've heard rumours, you see. Rumours about you. They say you're not up to scratch. Don't make the mark? Haven't got the stomach for it? They must have it wrong, surely. Oh, but have you heard the one about the useless egotist? Listen. He wanted to save the world, but he was so useless he ended up working in some dump where they think they change peoples' lives. Teaching a bunch of no hopers how to smell a flower and experience the wonder of nature through their nostrils. And he had dreamt of being the next Mandela. But there's more. Listen. The egotist worked his little socks off in the dump until, one day, he actually believed he was beginning to transcend his ego by becoming so very worthy and so very altruistic. He didn't need to save the world anymore. Now he had more humanity in him than that. It was no longer about recognition and glory, for that was all vanity and falling in love with one's own reflection. Narcissist! He'd risen above that now. Now he was truly inspired by the suffering of others. Until some bastard came along and made a mockery of all that, made his altruism look ridiculous, made him look ridiculous. For she showed him how easy it is to use people, to make them work for your own ends, to keep them under your absolute control, to make them massage your ego, to luxuriate in it all. She showed him that some of us are so very skilful at using others for ourselves, just as he had wanted to use others for his own egotistical glory. She constantly reminded him of how he had failed in his dreams and how she, under his very nose, was fulfilling hers with every single calculated word and action. Listen... Listen...

Chapter Sixteen

I was wound up to the hilt; blood racing through my veins like a billion fireflies, insane particles fizzing electrically across my brain. We held a Project meeting that weekend and I was still charged up like a murderer at the moment he finally knows he's about to plunge the knife. I really wanted to go on the next assignment and record Styles being an hour late for Exploring Leisure, but Jessica wanted to chip in. Billy wanted a crack as well, but it was decided that seventeen stone and six foot four was a dodgy lump to disguise. He said he didn't mind if Jessica went though, just as long as her disguise was guaranteed to protect her from being discovered. She got up on her toes and kissed him on the lips for that one, and for agreeing she should have the chance to make a personal contribution to The Project. Helen knocked up another belting disguise. Jessica was briefed to prioritise the avoidance of discovery, but to also try taking photos of the undergraduates in charge and of Styles getting off the train an hour late. Billy pointed out that technology was "bloody unbelievable these days," because Jessica had a phone which could take pictures whilst recording dates and times on them. I was encouraged by the thought that we might be starting to build up a significant weight of evidence against Styles. I was increasingly impatient to blow the whistle though.

Then, the following Tuesday, Jessica carried out her assignment. We all met at mine in the evening. She'd taken the photos, printed them off, arranged them tidily in a folder. Zebedee and I were tucking into the Jack Daniels, puffing cheroot smoke out through the skylight, and Helen was knocking back the still mineral water, when she arrived with Billy. We sat cross-legged on the floor, around my knackered old coffee table. Jessica opened her folder. She wasn't giggling at first.

"She didn't turn up until the end of the session, you know."

"You what?" I said, the whisky burning harsher on my tongue.

"Stepped off the train two hours late."

"What state were the students in by then?"

"Weren't exactly chilled out," she said. "You know how crucial it is for them, if they're expecting something to happen..."

"Like Styles being there when she says she's going to be?"

"Yes."

"Not that only being an hour late would have been acceptable anyway."

"Julian spent a lot of the time mumbling to himself. You know how he does when he's really stressed?"

"He didn't kick off, did he?" I asked, inclining my head expectantly.

"Thought he was going to at one point."

"How was Glenys?" said Zebedee.

"Biting into her hand again," said Jessica. "Really digging her teeth in, look," she held up a photo, so we could all check out Glenys treating her hand like a flapjack.

"You see," I said, standing, snatching the picture from her, holding it aloft like an example of heresy. "That's what she's doing to our guys! That's what she's doing to our vulnerable students!"

"Ok, Pete," said Helen, rising to take the photo from me. "Let's see what else Jess has got."

She looked into my eyes, dead straight. I slumped back to the floor. She turned to Jessica.

"Was everyone all right in the end?"

"Seemed well enough walking out of the station."

"Good. Do you have anything else?" asked Helen, sitting beside her on the carpet.

"A few with Josh and Rosie in charge. Can see they're a bit tense. Snapped these from the newsagents opposite. Pretending to read Cosmo and snapping when they weren't looking. Scary, but exciting. Felt like being in Bergerac."

"Bloody Bergerac?" said Billy, with laughing, dewy eyes.

"I know it's ancient, darling, but it's always on daytime telly. Seen a lot of daytime lately. One of Julian with chocolate cake all over his face," said Jessica, holding up a photo.

"Belter," I said. "What have you got of Styles getting off the train?"

"Ah, well. Had to slip a bit more undercover for these. Pulled my lapels right up over my ears."

"Hey, sugar, you really do get your kicks from Bergerac," quipped Zebedee, forming an 'O' with his mouth and biting off smoke rings in triplicate.

"Got her though. Three times. Look at these. Opening the train doors, stepping off, greeting Rosie with a hug."

"Yeah, that'd be right," I said, sarcastically.

"These are all right, aren't they?" asked Jessica, insecurity now weighing on her face.

"They're perfect, Jess. Absolutely perfect," said Helen, touching her shoulder.

"You sure you got dates and times on 'em all?" I asked.

"Course she is," said Billy.

"Right, time we grassed the bastard up, then."

Everyone watched me tip another shot into my glass and spark up one more cheroot. I stood and began pacing the room, like I'm Churchill addressing his war cabinet.

"Do you really reckon we've got enough...?" started Billy.

"What's the bother, Billy lad? There she is, ripping into the students at every turn, treating them like babies, undermining them to control them. And now she's neglecting 'em so much it's messing 'em up. All you need to do is look at Jessica's evidence. It's obvious. And we all know poor old Tony doesn't know his arse from his elbow anymore. Yet she can't bend over far enough for her precious undergraduate chums, can she? Squeezing every drop of use she can out of them. What she should be doing is teaching those she's been properly assigned to. Not putting 'em down to keep 'em under wraps, but building 'em up. Giving them something valuable, for fuck's sake!"

Helen, her head sort of quizzically tipped to one side, stared at me throughout a long pause.

"Come off it, you lot," I continued. "There's all this going on *and* she's taken a session out to supervise Josh, left some callow youth in charge. And now we've got the absolute proof that she's neglecting her students and putting them at risk. Photographic evidence, with times and dates, of her bowling up at the end of her own session, having left the undergraduates in charge of... oh, come on, it's time to hand her in to the council."

"Why did she have to see that university tutor on the morning of one of her sessions?" asked Zebedee.

"Do you really believe she was at a meeting with a university academic? Styles? I know she's clever but... no chance. It's all voluntary, this arrangement with Josh and Rosie, isn't it? They're volunteers, remember? Do you reckon Styles would take time out like that when she's not getting paid for it? I'll bet you she's moonlighting somewhere else though. I know that greedy bastard. I'll put my own money on it. That must be it, you know. That's why she wants to help 'em out so much. So she can use 'em to cover for her whilst she's off pulling a second wage. Talk about double time."

"Pete, you're pissed," said Jessica.

"I'm pissed off! Anyway, look, let's get back to it. We've got concrete, photographic evidence that she's threatening the well being of her students. And that is all we need."

"Pete?" said Helen.

"What?"

"We don't want the students subjected to her influence anymore than you do."

"Subjected to her influence," I said, mimicking her words.

"We can all see it's damaging to them. Why do you think we're involved in this? Listen, we're starting to make progress. And every piece of evidence we record is significant. I absolutely believe that, Pete. But I am of the opinion that we still need to be patient."

" 'I am of the opinion.' When you gonna lighten up, you? Eh?" I said, stopping my paces, standing over her. "I thought you were starting to chill a bit, enjoy yourself? You know about that? Enjoying yourself? You're reverting to type, Helen. We've got all we need. Just put your old set ways behind you, can't you? I mean, how many witness statements do you want us to write? There used to be a word for people like you at school, you know. I'm just trying to remember what... oh, that's it. Stiff. Stiff, that was it."

"Grow up, Pete," said Jessica.

I could feel the veins in my temples pounding away, but my pride and vanity had me attempting an air of cool which Zebedee might have aspired to. I blew a thin stream of cheroot smoke upwards and watched it break against the skylight glass. Helen stood to face me, rising up directly from her seated position on the floor, as straight as a pillar breaking through the earth's surface. I retreated back down into the depths of my armchair. I tried ignoring it, but the hurt crackling in her voice stung me like an icy wind.

"Ok, everyone. This is my opinion," she said. "We must be patient. We are now starting to gather more concrete evidence. Though this is not yet conclusive. We must press on. We have to be vigilant. But we do need more. Take this latest evidence. Deborah Styles could still claim an unforeseeable train delay. She might only receive a warning. And this would only alert her. Alert her to our activities. She would never reveal her true hand again. Yet, she would be free to neglect the students whenever she was sure she was not being watched. Our job is to protect the students in the longer term. What we need, before we blow the whistle, is enough evidence to make it stick. We must only make our move when we are absolutely certain that it is going to be conclusive."

Chapter Seventeen

I awoke the next morning properly rough. Guzzling a pint of orange juice, clinging to the desperate maxim that fresh air is a panacea, I pushed my head out through the skylight and into the day. To my left the sky was a canvas for wispy clouds tinged pink by a weakening sun, to my right, huge banks of darkening thunderclouds and the growing momentum of wind-swirled rain. The gathering storm.

An hour or so later, by the time the sessions kicked off at Back Road, the storm was hurling weather at our town and all the 'out in the community' courses had been transferred indoors. Back Road was jam-packed. So much so that we had to fold away the mobile partitions to create more space. From my Literacy session with Anna I could see everybody else in the main hall. Jessica and Billy were taking Computers, Zebedee was researching the history of British choral music with a quartet of acolytes. Helen was absolutely committed to her Art class, but we kept glancing at each other across the void and awkwardly averting our eyes.

Styles was supposed to be teaching her proper students but they'd been palmed off onto a learning support assistant, who was doing her best at getting them to move a ball around and imagine it 'heavy', 'cold', 'stinky'. The students thought this was hilarious and their screeched shouting suggested there might be a riot on. The LSA looked very flustered. Especially when the ball kept flying off course and bouncing into neighbouring sessions. She was having a job coping and her face and neck had turned hot pink under the stress of it all.

Styles was in a separate room, poring over portfolios with the undergraduates. It was a room between the main hall, Margaret's office and the kitchen, and so a conduit for everyone. Consequently, its doors were kept open for convenience, which allowed me to glimpse her through shifting spaces in the student gaggle.

I'd just set Anna up with another exercise when Margaret walked into the hall from the office. She was 'doing her rounds,' as she called it, dipping into each session to touch base with the students. I watched her moving around the room in what had become a consistently stuttering manner. She'd hang back from a session, lingering at its edges, unsure about when to step forward to show an interest. Like the new kid at school whose desperation for acceptance is constantly being overridden by the fear of rejection. A year earlier there was no questioning her status, her authority. Most importantly, *she* hadn't questioned it. Now you could see the doubt etched in deepening lines across her face, seeping into her body language and speech patterns. Styles had, of course, stepped in to offer solace and Margaret had clung on, as Styles very well knew she would. And I just knew her predicament was being exacerbated by Styles' exploiting her for her own interests. We were witnessing this exploitation again in Styles' use of the undergraduates, an arrangement originally approved by Margaret. But, that day at Back Road, the issue was heightened by Margaret allowing Styles to supervise Josh and Rosie, in front of the rest of us, whilst an LSA struggled to run one of her council courses. You could tell by Margaret's manner how self-conscious she was about it.

However, that just demonstrated to me how much control and power Styles now had over her. At least Styles' latest actions smacked of an arrogance which showed she had no suspicions about our intentions to shop her to the council. But for her to brazenly supervise the undergraduates whilst leaving her students high and dry? For her to do that so blatantly in full view of the rest of us, after what had already happened? There had to be a reason which was very important to her.

Margaret was now edgily waiting beside Helen's Art class. Helen ensured all the students were engaged and then invited her to come closer, summarising for her the general activity and outlining the differentiated work set out for individual learners. Formerly, Margaret would have pulled up a chair and got stuck in, confidently dipping paintbrushes, applying colours with a flourish, encouraging the students to experiment and express themselves. But now her involvement was reduced to looking over shoulders and saying, "That's good... oh, now that's good, isn't it?... Isn't that good?" She was still devoted to the students but it was like she'd forgotten how to properly feel that devotion, as if she'd been slightly removed from it.

A raucous laugh pitched across the hall. A guffaw. Heads turned instinctively before returning to their work. I locked my eyes on Styles. She had her back to me, it was shaking with mirth. Josh and Rosie were trying to focus on their portfolios but they kept covering their mouths, attempting to hold down the laughter. Styles was clasping their arms in a show of trying to control the hilarity. They were like the naughty kids at the back of the classroom, consumed by group bonding, utterly disrespectful.

"That's good, Anna," said Margaret.

She was standing behind us, a pace away.

"We're doing speech marks today. When somebody speaks, you put speech marks. Yeah, yeah. Like this. Speech marks," said Anna.

"That's really good, Anna."

"Yeah, yeah. I've got the moves, haven't I Pete?"

"You've got the moves, Anna."

"That's really good, Pete."

"Cheers, Margaret. Margaret, I need a word."

At mid morning break, she nodded at me from behind the security of the 'conduit room' door jamb. I walked purposefully through the crowded hall and past the Art group.

"Carefully, Pete," said Helen, probably sensing the tautness in my body.

Margaret lead the way through the conduit room.

"Everything all right, Marge?" asked Styles.

"Fine and dandy, ta," I said, taking a shot at equilibrium, not stopping, not daring to look at her for fear of what I might give away.

I followed Margaret into the office and closed the door. We sat in shiny revolving chairs, on opposite sides of her table, just as we had at interview. As we had all those times when she'd taken me to one side to offer reassurance and self-belief. When she'd been strong and energetic and filled with passion for what she was doing for so many people. Now her eyes were rheumy, as if she'd been crying all night. Dazed, the life wrung from them, they looked out at me.

"What's up, Margaret?" I said.

"What's up?" she said, gazing through me.

"You looking after yourself?"

"An apple a day, fags only after meals."

"Down to twenty meals a day now, then? Bum bum."

"Mmm?"

I listened to the storm crashing around, a windowpane away.

"I know what you're all saying about me," she said, eyes suddenly alert.

"Come off it."

"That I've sold you down the swanny, that I don't give a stuff about you."

"Who says that we say that?"

"Because all I care about is A number one? Isn't that right?"

"Who says that we say that?" I said, leaning forward, wanting her to confirm it was Styles who'd been winding her up.

"I've seen your faces, huddled around, talking. Oh, I still know what goes on here."

"We're concerned for you. That's how we really feel. Do you understand why we're concerned, Margaret?"

"Why would you be bothered about me?" she said, slouching slightly, as if the question was weighing her down.

"After all you've done for me, I reckon I'm pretty well qualified to answer that."

"Whatever you've done you've done for yourself, lad."

I looked into her eyes, trying to capture what lay behind

them.

"Margaret, you're an amazing person."

"I still know what goes on here. I know what you're all saying."

She stared vacantly at the rain streaming down the windowpane.

"Is there anyone else here who reckons they know what we're saying?" I asked.

"What do you mean by that?" she said, sharply.

A pause.

"Why are you here, Pete?"

"Remember when stuff's been on my mind? When my head's been totally mashed and I've come to you? Because you listen and you help and you make people believe in themselves?"

"What are you getting at?"

"You rescued me, Margaret."

"You did that for yourself."

"You saved me because you believed in me. And I trusted you."

"But you don't trust me anymore."

"No... No... I do trust you. Of course I do. That's why I've come to you. Can you assure me that whatever we talk about now is confidential? That nobody else will hear about what we're going to discuss?"

"You trust me, do you?" she asked, smiling wryly.

"Why do you even have to ask me that?"

"Because you're seeking my reassurance. If you trust me, why do you need my reassurance? I'm still the person I was.

No matter what they all say. I'm still the person I've always been," she said, chin trembling.

"Of course. Of course."

"Nobody can take that from me."

"That's right, Margaret. Nobody. Not one single person can take that from you," I said, furrowing my brow.

A pause.

"What do you want from me, Pete?"

"Why isn't Deborah teaching her class today?"

"Deborah, is it? Don't think I didn't know what this was about," she said, sitting up taller, like this was the real business now.

"I know she's trying to help Rosie and Josh but... I mean, have you seen poor Caroline out there? She's doing her best, but have you seen..."

"Caroline is a very capable learning support."

"It's not her class though, is it? Not her responsibility. Deborah should be teaching her own students, not helping Rosie and Josh with their portfolios."

"She can still keep an eye on her session. That door's always open."

"Oh come off it, Margaret. She's got her back to the door, anyway."

"I don't know what you all have against Deborah. She's an excellent teacher, with a wealth of experience..."

"She tell you that, did she?" I quickly asked, suddenly riled by the unjust plaudits.

"I've seen her record."

"Written in tablets of stone, was it? Special delivery from

behind a burning bush on Mount Sinai, was it?"

"Jealousy can be very destructive, Pete."

"Jealousy?"

A long deep pause.

"Listen, blame me, all of you," she said. "I created this mess. If only I'd... look, I'm sorry. Blame me, please blame me. But not Deborah. Leave the woman alone. She's just trying to do her job."

"She's not doing her job though, is she? Why won't you hear a word against her?"

"She's the only one who's been there for me."

"And why do you think that is?"

"What do you mean?"

"You can't see it at all."

"See what?"

The stormy skies lashed another squall against the window, whisking away my thoughts momentarily before they settled again.

"Does the council know about the undergraduates?" I asked.

"Yes," she said, defensively.

"Are you sure?"

"Do you trust me, Pete?"

"Ok, sorry. And are they happy about the arrangement?"

She tried to laugh it off.

"Of course. Why shouldn't they be? *They're* not paying her for supervising..."

Then she realised what she'd just given away.

"The university *are* paying her? I knew it!" I said, both

enraged and triumphant, thumping the table. "I bloody knew she'd be pulling a second wage!"

"Pete, listen."

"That explains everything. I bet the council don't know about her pulling two wages at once, do they?" I was half laughing now.

"No..."

"I'll bet you haven't let on, have you?"

A long pause.

"Listen, Pete, Deborah has extensive experience, both as a teacher and as a supervisor. I have absolute confidence in her abilities to fulfil both responsibilities simultaneously," said Margaret, trying to hide behind a show of professionalism.

But by now I'd lost all sympathy. Any final drops of warmth had been frozen out. It felt like there was ice in my guts. My face was stone cold.

"She's exploiting you, Margaret," I said.

"Don't be ridiculous," she said, turning away slightly.

"That's what she does. She manipulates everyone."

"She's done nothing but give since she's been here."

"No. She plays that game. She's very clever at giving that impression."

"Don't be ridiculous."

"But she only gives to get as much as she can for herself."

"I want you out of my office now, please."

"There's not an ounce of altruism in her, Margaret."

"Out, please."

She stood and started moving to the door.

"Are you getting a cut?" I said.

She stopped abruptly.

"What did you say?"

"She slipping you a cut from her university pay?"

"Why are you speaking like that?"

"What's your percentage, Marge?"

"Not me. No, that's wrong," she said, slowly turning to face me.

"No, you wouldn't do that."

"Back Road, not me."

"Back Road?"

"Financially, we're still... "

"How much?"

"Deborah's been kind enough..."

"How much?"

"To donate..."

"How much?"

"Twenty percent."

"Twenty?"

"Every penny's crucial."

"She's keeping you sweet."

Chapter Eighteen

At four o'clock we all piled into the Cock and Bottle for a Project meeting. The old geezer, drinking Guinness from a metal tankard, was leaning against the bar in his medal-adorned blazer.

"How do, Pop," said Zebedee, springing up to the bar.

"How do, Pup," said the old man, instantly smiling.

"What's yer poison?" said Zebedee, pulling a twenty from a golden bicycle clip.

"Oh dat's voery koind o' yer, so it is. I'oll 'ave anudder point o' de black stuff," said the old man, tittering to himself, medals merrily clinking.

"Rioght ya are, sir. So you are, so you will, so you do."

This time Jessica actually giggled at Zebedee buying a round on borrowed money. We set up the pool table and Zebedee lit up the jukebox with some deep south blues. Jessica teamed up with him and Billy said he'd ref. so that Helen could have a bash and partner me. Zebedee, imagining putting as much weight behind it as Minnesota Fats, cracked open the pack from the break off. Soon, to a soundtrack of lamenting blues and clicking pool balls, we were discussing the latest.

"Did a spot of earwigging today," said Jessica, excitedly.

"What you got?" I asked.

"Country Life group, next Thursday. Off to Darley Valley. Meet at the Gorge Cafe at ten. Oh bollocks. Missed."

"Head up, lass, head up," said Billy.

"Glenys and Kerry researching it on the internet today."

"I'll take that one," I said. "I'm not working Thursday morning and I know the place."

"I'd like to come with you," said Helen, lining up a long shot.

"You're working, aren't you?" I said.

"Margaret owes me some holiday. I should be able to arrange a qualified supply teacher to cover for me," she said, whacking a distant 'stripe' into the back of a pocket.

"Should I come round to yours this weekend, then?" I asked, as casually as I could.

"Why?"

"Try out some disguises?"

She took her time, carefully eyeing up options for her next shot.

"I'm busy this weekend," she eventually said.

"Washing her hair!" laughed Jessica.

"You can come over one evening next week," said Helen, delicately sliding in a plant.

"Sound. Yeah. All right, then," I said, staring at the wooden floor, shuffling my feet.

"I'll let you know when it's convenient."

"Yeah. Sound."

Zebedee, Jessica and Billy were casting glances and smirking at each other. I edged closer to the jukebox, my pool cue a crutch, and flicked through some choices.

"Owt good, lad?" said Billy.

"Eh? Listen, there's something... oh, Helen, finish your shot."

She slammed in another stripe and screwed back for the

choice of two more.

"Fuck me," I said.

"Adrenalin," she said.

"Look, I've found out why Styles is using Rosie and Josh in the way she is."

They leaned towards me over the pool table, their hair shiny beneath shaded light.

"I got it out of Margaret today. I hope I didn't crack her up any more, but she let it slip. Styles is pulling another wage. The university is actually paying her for this undergraduate supervising. I knew it, I'm telling you, I knew it was money! She's grabbing two wages at once. I'm in there thinking no wonder she's neglecting her proper students when she's got these financial obligations to the university. She's getting paid to ensure Josh and Rosie complete their portfolios and meet their case study deadlines."

"You think that meeting with Mrs Lee was legit on Tuesday, then?" said Zebedee.

"Sounds like it."

"This has got to count as a significant cornerstone of our case against her," said Helen. "Surely the council don't know about this."

"They know she's supervising, but they've no idea she's getting paid for it and the impact that's having on her proper students. And neither do they know about her handing over twenty percent every month to Back Road just to keep Margaret sweet."

"No way," said Jessica.

"You reckon we're getting close to blowing the whistle

yet, Helen?" I said.

She got us to stand back before she stunned in another stripe. She slowly chalked her cue tip, blew away the blue dust.

"Ok. Obviously we're getting close. I think we should hold on for just a few more days. We'll make sure that at least one of us is watching each 'out and about' session to ensure student safety. Ten days should give me enough time to get all the evidence absolutely watertight. And, the way she's going, we should be able to gather enough additional stuff in that time to enhance our case. Remember as well that we put in pay claims to the council in ten days time. I'm thinking she's going to claim for that session she didn't turn up for on Tuesday. It might only be one session but it will be tantamount to fraud, and it will back up our feelings about her dishonesty."

She stretched one leg along the length of the pool table rail, bridged over an awkward cluster and, with a resounding crack, wellied in another stripe.

Chapter Nineteen

We spied on Styles for the next week or so, as she carried on supervising the undergraduates at the expense of her proper students. We recorded it all and handed it to Helen, who puit it in order and catalogued it, fattening up the Project portfolio. It just got on my nerves though, all this biding our time. We gathered more evidence, but it was more of the same. It felt like the iron had been hot when the two wages and twenty percent thing had been confirmed. It felt like we should have struck then and that now our chances were hissing away in a barrel of iced water. But Helen stayed strong, insisting that patience for a few more days, and Styles' anticipated fraudulent pay claim, could prove crucial. I drank a lot that week, spent a couple of late ones at 'Stanleys' grubby old dive. Even pulled once. I put everything into escaping my ego and the deepening threat posed to it by Styles. But the stupor of drink or sex is forever a transitory escape; you are always left with a stonking hangover, stained sheets and, in my case, an increasingly besieged ego.

At seven the following Thursday morning, disguised as a seasoned rambler, I jumped into my decayed eleven hundred and drove up through the valley and into the remote village. I was meeting Helen at the stables, where she keeps Tess and Durberville. Then we were off back down the valley a bit, for a fry up at the Country Life group's meeting place, the Gorge Cafe. I parked in the Crown car park, creaked on the handbrake and started walking towards the wide expanse of moorland heather.

"Muffle muffle muffle, Sir!" said the landlord, leaning out of an upstairs window, his belly settling lazily on the sill.

"Morning, landlord. Am I all right parked here for half an hour?" I said, approaching.

"Oh it's you, muffle. Didn't muffle you then. Aye, lad, aye."

"You sure you're not Santa?"

"Ho ho ho."

"How's grouse season?"

"Glorious, lad. Muffling glorious."

"I'll drink to that, landlord. Cheers."

As I turned I could hear him tittering under that thick facial thatch. And I sensed his big belly wobbling as he spoke.

"Nice beard, lad."

"Cheers, landlord."

"Ho ho ho. Hee hee hee."

I moved along the peaty pathways, which crisscrossed the acres of bunched purple heather like the burnt markings of God's giant brander, ancient scars embedded deep into the moor's pitted skin. As I approached the stables, grouse called out serenely; 'chut chut chut.' And there was Helen in jodhpurs, grooming Durberville, firmly smoothing him shiny. And there's me, like a prick, shouting.

"Morning, Helen!"

Durberville immediately spooked, skittishly side stepping and kicking up his hooves. But Helen, as calm as a doldrums sea, spoke soft words to him, soothed him in gentle tones, massaged his neck, slowly rubbed below his ears. And he settled under her warmth, the steamed breath coming from his nostrils emanating evenly again. I watched her movements and there was no hint of annoyance towards me, no thoughts about me or herself. Just a quiet focus on Durberville because, for those moments, he needed her. And that's what she's like. If someone needs her, she doesn't think about herself, she helps. That's it. She beckoned me over. I moved tentatively towards them. Quietly reassuring Durberville, she took my hand and carefully placed it beside his mane, encouraging me to stroke.

When she'd mucked out at the stables and changed into some keen rambler's clobber, we headed off to the Gorge Cafe for a slap up Traditional English. Running deep behind the cafe is the gorge itself and, after breakfast, we sat on a bench overlooking it, awaiting the arrival of the Country Life group. I had my phone ready to take pictures of any neglect, and Helen had notepaper and a pen blue-tacked to the inside of an ordinance survey map. We were perfectly poised to record further evidence. But all I could think about was the end of tomorrow, the day when all this recording would stop and we'd be ready to blow the whistle.

Recent deluges meant that water burst through the gorge beneath us, whipping up spray on the breeze to cool our faces, yet simultaneously bubbling over rocks like a potion in a cauldron. Hewn into the gorge's moss-covered sides are deep, tall ledges which are now used as fenced in pathways for visitors, in order that they may experience the gorge in full, dramatic proximity. To enter these pathways visitors must cross a bridge spanning the gorge. We fixed our eyes on the bridge.

Firstly, we heard Kerry, Glenys and Stevo singing 'hiho, hiho, it's off to work we go,' then we saw them all slowly appearing on the bridge, moving in single file.

Rosie... Julian... Tony... Glenys... Kerry... Stevo... Josh

"Where's Snow White?" I said. "Where is Styles, Helen?"

And we watched the space behind Josh widen, and we heard Kerry, Glenys and Stevo still singing, excitement soaking up fear, and we saw Tony inspecting the bridge for reasons of health and safety, and we saw the space behind Josh still widening.

"Late again," I said.

"Take a picture. Keep gathering evidence. Right up until the end. You're shaking. Deep breaths," said Helen.

The group of seven walked along the pathways, exploring the gorge. From our vantage point, we looked down into the chasm. Soon they were too deep in the earth for us to hear their voices above the rushing water and so we just kept watching. I tried to focus through the blurring spray, to think about their well being, to care about their safety. And I remember seeing Kerry and Glenys tickling Stevo, and Stevo screaming in mock protest, when what he really meant was 'tickle me more.' And I remember Josh and Rosie stopping the group and trying to look authoritative, wagging fingers in callow attempts at discipline. I remember seeing the undergraduates properly kakking it, under the sheer weight of responsibility thrust upon them. And we didn't doubt that the fenced in pathways were safe, otherwise we'd have been down there pulling the group out, giving the game away, course we would. But I still should have been thinking about those seven. All of them vulnerable.

"They are safe down there, you know," said Helen, gently clasping my arm.

"Mmm?"

"I know the owners. They do their checks every day. Those fenced in pathways are one hundred percent secure. There's no need to worry about them."

Pause.

"Where is the bastard?" I said.

"We'll watch over them and tomorrow we'll be ready."

"She's laughing at us."

"But you don't have to worry about her anymore," she said. "From next week, she'll no longer be working with our students. I promise you."

"She's mocking us."

Pause.

"You know what she loves most?" I said, turning to her, my eyes fixed on hers.

"What's that?"

"That we hate her and that we suffer. Our hatred for her half kills us, but she loves our hate. Can you hear that? She actually loves that we hate her. She needs absolute control to sustain her ego, and what more powerful sense of control could someone have than loving the fact they're hated? Loving that it half kills us to hate her, but that we're powerless to do anything about it!"

"Do you really hate her, Pete?"

Pause.

"Everyone feeling hatred inside has the power to do

something about it," she said.

"And where did you read that?"

"Don't mock me."

"Look, if someone truly hates," I said. "They don't think 'today I am experiencing hatred, yet it is within my power to do something about it.'"

"Some people do."

"Bollocks."

"What do they say, then?"

"They say ..."

"What?"

"I HATE!"

I remember the seven faces jerking up at us, like a moment of choreographed melodrama in a musical. But Helen kept calm in her hiker's disguise, held up her hands to the group in apology, played out the role of castigating me with an ordinance survey strike across the chest. The Country Life group again began moving slowly along the pathways, as I scanned the bridge once more for any sign of Styles and Helen lined me up for a good talking to.

"Pete, listen to me. It's important that you listen. Let's not throw it away now. Remember, after tomorrow's sessions, she'll put in her pay claims. She'll almost certainly claim for the times when she hasn't been teaching. And we have photographic evidence as proof. And remember that tomorrow we'll be ready to present every piece of telling evidence we've gathered to the council. If we give ourselves away now she's bound to learn of it. What do you think she'll do? Lie down? No chance. You know her, don't you? She'll ready herself with excuses, wriggle out of it. And there'll be no fraudulent pay claims going in. The whole Project will collapse. Everything we've worked for."

"I know you're right, but..."

"No 'buts,' Pete. We must stay professional until the very end. Don't forget we're doing this for the well being of our students. We can't jeopardize that. This is for them."

"I know..."

"This is not a personal battle."

I remember being properly wound up by that. But, as I felt those heated particles ricocheting around in my skull and my heart protesting vehemently against a caged existence, I remember thinking how much she knew me already, how much she understood. I wanted to escape it. But I was too far gone for that now.

For the next two hours, beneath the cover of disguise, we stayed close to the group as they explored in and around the gorge. I kept trying to listen to the voice in my head, the one telling me to think of the students, the one which said we'd be ready to blow the whistle tomorrow, the one which calmly reminded me of my professional obligations. But my feral instinct gripped me ever tighter. I was constantly scanning the landscape for any sign of Styles. And the particles blew white-hot, and the blood pumped viscerally, and the miniature drummer slammed away at my temples. Two hours. No show. Again. No fucking show!

We watched the seven move off in their taxis. Helen put away her ordinance survey map. I ripped off my beard. We both had sessions to teach at Back Road in the afternoon, but there was enough time.

"There's a place I want to show you," I said.

I drove the eleven hundred a bit further down the valley, to a place where a road ascends and weaves along the valley top. I parked up and we moved carefully down the sheer valley side, along the zigzag pathway, gripping tufts of grass. I showed her the two blocks of square rock and there we stood, in the gap between them, looking out across the valley.

"Is this your private place?" she asked.

"Welcome to my veranda."

"Do you serve cocktails?"

"Did you hide under the covers when you were a kid?" I asked. "When there was a storm outside?"

"Oh, yes."

"And it was scary, because it felt like you were actually inside the storm. But it was more exciting than scary because, though you felt daring, you knew you were safe?"

"I remember that feeling," she said.

"I think I've been like that all my life. Wanting to be daring but, all the time, knowing I'm safe."

"And that's why you come here?"

"You really know me, don't you?"

"I'm not sure."

Pause.

"Do you reckon everybody has an ego?" I said.

"Not sure."

"I was in India once. Look!"

I pointed towards a sparrowhawk soaring above and put a shoulder to her cheek, so she could sight along my stretched out arm.

"Sparrowhawk," I said.

"Beautiful."

"A bird of prey followed me around India. I don't mean in disguise."

She laughed.

"I mean, whenever I looked up, there was one of these birds there. I thought it meant something. You think I'm a maniac, don't you?"

"Maybe," she said, smiling at me.

"I thought it was telling me something, that's all."

"What? What was it telling you?"

"To help people. You know, to be truly altruistic."

"You mean, like you do now?"

"Well, no, not... no."

"I don't understand."

"Thousands of people. Millions of people."

"What?"

"Nationwide. Worldwide."

We watched the sparrowhawk drift away on the wind.

"I am a maniac. Egomaniac," I said.

I was embarrassed now, revealing too much. I was like the kid again, wanting to escape under the covers. I tried to focus on the valley, looking to be seduced by its breeze, wishing I hadn't brought her here, not even understanding why I had. But I could sense the intensity of her eyes searching out my attention.

"Question," she said. "Do egomaniacs hate being egomaniacs? You're claiming to be one, but it sounds like you hate it."

"I do hate it."

"But I always thought egomaniacs loved it. Don't they love being egomaniacs?"

"I hate it."

Pause.

"You helped me," she said.

"Don't be soft. You're brilliant at everything."

"I can hold my own in the classroom, maybe. I know how to care for horses. Those familiar situations make *me* feel safe. But I relied on them too much before... before I got to know you. I needed them to compensate for everything that was lacking. But you trusted me, you believed in me. And I admired you, because you wanted to fight for what was right. I thought, this person I admire really believes in me. And the confidence that gave me, I can't describe it."

"But I admire you too."

And the seductive breeze was curling around the blocks of rock, and around our necks. And, when we kissed, particles fizzed in my brain and my blood pulsed maniacally, yet my skin was refreshed, as if by a gentle wave rippling, emanating from the base of my spine, spreading slowly out to my fingertips. And, in the midst of it all, the heat and the cool, the sun and the shade, it felt like I was luxuriating in one long, slow, indulgent stretch. Except I didn't want to move, to escape. I wanted to stay there on our veranda, sipping cocktails, falling in love.

Chapter Twenty

The next day, the last of our spying on Styles, was the day when we could stop gathering evidence, the day when she would put in her fraudulent pay claims, the day when we'd be poised to get the bastard sacked. I awoke that morning relieved at the thought, yet as taut as one of Zebedee's guitar strings. In a few hours we'd be ready to knock on the council's heavy oak door, armed with our big fat Project portfolio. But what if she got away with it?

We sent Billy out, with shades and tache, in his own eleven hundred rusty bucket, on the Project's final assignment. He was charged with staking out the church hall, a couple of streets away from Back Road, to see if Styles would bother showing for her Drama sessions. The rest of us were at Back Road that morning and Jessica, receiving text updates from Billy in his motor, kept us filled in on the latest. At morning break, outside in fag-time corner, Zebedee, Helen and I huddled around Jessica's phone and read Billy's full message catalogue.

"J and R just showed up. Holding portfolios. Waiting outside door. Where's Styles??? Me? Not used to being crammed in car too long. Sardine! X"

"Students here now. X"

"Bloody sardine! More fish in sea? Naa. You're the one for me, lass. X"

"Still no Styles... X"

"Students rehearsing on doorstep. Stevo on one knee, Glenys looking other way, hard to get, Kerry tugging on

Glenys' arm, he's not worth it, Julian standing guard, dreaming of sticky toffee pudd wi' orange custard, Tony trying to put his jumper under Stevo's knee, health and safety. X"

"Bloody hell! Styles here! And on time! X"

"All in church hall now. Will keep eye out. Sardine? It's no life. What's on menu for toneet anyhow, lass? Friday neet sweet??? X"

Billy stayed undercover for the rest of the morning, seeing nobody leave the church hall and growing increasingly uncomfortable in his cramped up state. At lunchtime we gathered once more for cigarettes and read his latest text.

"Lunch now. All still inside. Styles stayed put. Me like a trussed up chicken in a Billycan. Further instructions? X!"

"Something tells me the big man wants out o' that gig," said Zebedee.

And it was at that moment we decided to pull the plug on the spying. So we let Billy come away from there. I mean, there was no more evidence to gather. Styles was suitably ensconced. We were set to blow the whistle. So we let him go. What happened next, I learnt from the people who'd been there. I can't remember who told me what. It just came in snippets, from various sources, and I pieced it together.

After Billy's left the scene, everyone's buzzing around inside, getting ready for a good feed. Rosie and Josh are in charge of lunch prep and today they're proud and excited and a bit more confident. More confident because they're on some familiar ground, rustling up an old undergrad staple, stir-fry. They've even brought in their own wok, they're that proud and excited. Styles is there, giving them a last minute pep talk no doubt, to keep them sweet and motivated and bended to her will, as she gets ready to leave the building. And then, sometime between twelve and half past, just after Billy's driven off, Styles says "bye bye, now be good for Josh and Rosie," and leaves the undergraduates in charge. She exits the building, gets in her car and she's off. Only, she doesn't exit by the front door. She's only two streets from Back Road and she's afraid of being spotted. So she exits by the back door. Which is the fire exit door. But the fire exit swings open all the time if it's not locked. And so, to close it, you have to lock it. Then, of course, you can't let yourself back in without the key. And, when she comes back, she doesn't want to risk being spotted re-entering the building using the front door. So, when she's locked the fire door, she takes the key with her.

Afterwards, we were all saying why didn't she lock the door and leave the key with Josh and Rosie, to put back in the lock on the inside, then phone them to let her in when she returned. Afterwards, we were all saying why didn't she get Josh or Rosie to check the coast was clear outside the front door. Afterwards, we were all saying why didn't she wear a big floppy hat and sunglasses. But, afterwards, people always say stuff like that. There's always a more sensible way. A more responsible way. And, afterwards, people nearly always realise that it happened because somebody was being stupid or fucking irresponsible.

So Styles has jumped ship. Kerry, Glenys, Stevo, Julian, Tony et al are sitting around a big round table, in the middle of a church hall, devouring Josh and Rosie's lovely stir-fry. Josh and Rosie are beaming proudly, as the compliments float seductively through the air, under their noses and into their ears. The two callow chefs are relaxing, relaxing, relaxing, amid the tempting atmosphere of culinary success. The dish, a triumph! They return to the kitchen to refill each bowl with a second helping. The wok, a cauldron, slowly simmering. But that's the way they always leave it in the Halls of Residence; make up a big old wok full, leave it gently simmering. Everyone helps themselves, whenever they return from a lecture or a seminar or a tutorial. And the person who spoons out the last bowlful turns off the heat. "Sometimes, it's hours before the last bowlful's gone," I heard Josh say, afterwards. And now the undergraduates are beaming in the afterglow, they are so pleased to have shared some of their own world with that of their 'students for the afternoon,' they are so contented with the pleasure they have given and the rewards of gratitude they have received. They are infused with confidence, fired up with enthusiasm for the afternoon drama session, they feel like they could do justice to a Shakespearean tragedy.

Rosie and Josh are keen to get the drama started. The detritus of lunch is cleared. The wok still simmers. The last bowlful has not yet been taken. It is force of habit. The kitchen door is closed. It is forgotten. It is forgotten that the only way to the front door is through the kitchen.

Afterwards, the caretaker said he'd checked the fire alarm the month before. Gerry, the chief fire officer, asked him when he'd last changed the batteries. "They have to run out sometime," said Gerry.

Afterwards, as Rosie bawled her eyes out, she admitted that Tony had wanted to check throughout the building 'for reasons of health and safety.' But they'd dismissed it, because Tony always talked about health and safety and they'd been told to discourage this 'obsessive' behaviour of his.

I remember Margaret bursting in on our afternoon sessions at Back Road, phone in her hand, despair in her voice.

"They're in a fire! At St. Martin's! Josh and Rosie and the students!"

"Where's Styles?" I said.

"Where's Deborah?" Penny yelled into the phone. "Haircut? She's gone for a haircut!" she screamed.

We were out of our chairs at that point, shouting at a couple of teachers to stay put as we headed for the door.

"Right, Josh, calm down a minute. Listen to me," said Margaret, sounding more in command now than we'd heard her in months. "Are you all together? Ok. Now, calmly, make your way to the fire exit. You know, it's at the back of the building."

Jessica was on the blower to Billy, telling him to get back to the church hall, sharpish.

"She's what? Taken the key?" said Margaret.

We were out of the door now, pelting it down the street. I could hear Margaret behind us on her mobile, battling to breath evenly, trying to talk Josh through it.

"We're just around the corner, Josh. Now, the fire's in the kitchen?... But, don't you have to go through the kitchen to get to the front door?... Ok, Josh, try to stay calm. For the other guys. Ok, listen to me. Is it safe to get past the fire?... Come on, Josh, is it actually a big fire, or is it still very small?... You can hear what?... Crackling?"

"Have they called 999?" Helen shouted over her shoulder.

"Have you called 999, Josh? Have you called 999?"

But then, as we turned the final corner, we heard the sirens coming.

It paralysed us, seeing that terrible inferno. The kitchen window like the opening to a furnace, flames licking around the roof eves, the smoke black, thick, choking, encroaching on the rest of the building. The sirens came closer, a repeatedly screamed renting of the air, closer... closer... closer.

"Josh, can you hear the sirens?" asked Margaret. "Yes, they're just around the corner. Get as far away from the fire as possible. How are the guys?... Yes, well keep reassuring them... You can do it, Josh. You can do it. Can you hear the sirens?... They're nearly here. You can do it, Josh!"

Margaret's increasingly desperate exhortations snapped us suddenly from paralysis. We were like sprinters hearing the starting gun, about to hammer it around the back to see if there was any way we could batter down that fire door. But then the engines wailed around the last corner and chief fire officer, Gerry, was leaning out of the first one, shouting.

"Stay back! Stay back!"

Most of the crew started setting up, unravelling hoses, assessing the target area. Two men unhooked a battering ram from the first engine. Gerry began talking very clearly and very calmly into his mobile phone. But not to Josh.

"Ok, Tony, we're here now. The lads are just setting up the hoses. Ok, Tony, listen to me. Have you got everybody to the back of the building?... Have you accounted for everybody?... Good, Tony. Are you all waiting by the fire door?... Good... Yes, Tony, having everyone lying on the ground is the correct procedure. Well done, mate. Now, is there smoke where you are?... It's coming in. Ok, Tony, you're doing really well. Me and Mick and Johno are coming around the back now. We've got a battering ram, Tony."

We all pegged it after them.

"Ok, Tony. Now I want you to make sure everyone is clear of the fire door... Well done, mate... You made sure nobody opened the kitchen door? Brilliant job, Tony... Yes, you're right, oxygen is fuel to the flames... Yes, mate, you've given everybody an extra fifteen minutes there. Now, don't speak anymore. Just concentrate on breathing calmly. Right, Tony, are you ready?... Ok, we're coming in."

Some crawled out on their hands and knees, spluttering after the first taste of smoke inhalation. Some were crying. Some had faces frozen with shock. Kerry... Glenys... Julian... Stevo... Josh... Rosie... And Tony, last out, with all accounted for.

"Is that everybody, Tony?" asked Gerry.

Helen, to make sure, took the register from Rosie and checked it against the smoke-smudged faces.

"Everyone's here," she said.

The lads tackling the fire had now all but extinguished it. We trudged back around the front, like something out of 'Dulce et Decorum est,' to a grassed area across the road from the burnt building. The paramedics did their work, doing their checks, asking their questions. We all mucked in where we could; comforting, reassuring. Billy came back. The fire was out. The acrid smell of the aftermath clung to the air.

I had my arm around Stevo.

"Eh up, Stevo."

"Eh up, Peto."

"Belting to see you, pal. How you doing?"

"Belting to see *you*, pal."

"Eh up, Stevo, eh up."

"Eh up, Peto."

Zebedee was next to us, softening the trauma for Julian.

"Huge sponge cakes, dude. New Orleans Mardi Gras. Now that's where you'll get some proper feed, man. Yeah, man. Those big ol' jazz bands marching, all that razzmatazz. And all you have to do is lie back, soak it up and stuff your face with blueberry pie and big ol' burgers!"

"With ketchup and mustard and gherkins and mayonnnnaaaiiiise?" said Julian.

"Yeah, dude, yeah," said Zebedee.

Stevo raised his eyebrows at me, tried a smile.

"Eh up, Stevo. Eh up, lad."

Jessica was sitting nearby on the grass with Billy, whose massive shoulders were shaking.

"Were you to know what was going to happen?" she said.

He pinched the top of his nose, dug thick fingers into the corners of his eyes.

"Billy," she said. "Glenys and Kerry over there. Come on, darling."

As she stood, Billy looked up at her so intently I almost reckoned on his love for her levitating him, like some Hindu deity, from the ground. They floated over to Glenys and Kerry. I watched them for a while. They were concerned, intent on the well being of others, thoughts of themselves now evaporating in the dirtied air.

Tony was walking slowly around the periphery of the grassed area with Gerry. They had their hands behind their backs, very earnest expressions on their faces. They looked like Churchill and Montgomery in the gardens of a North African embassy, at a time when Monty was just starting to turn the tide on Rommel. Tony had turned the tide inside the church hall. He'd smelt the smoke, alerted the others, heard the century old dried out wooden units crackling, asserted that the kitchen door must remain shut, when Rosie and Josh's unthinking instinct was to feast the blaze on a shit load more oxygen. He'd given the order for everyone to walk calmly to the back of the building by the fire door, so they could be easily located from the outside. He'd used his own 'contingency' phone to call 999. He'd accurately described the burning building, its location, the exact coordinates of the group's position inside. He'd insisted everyone lay on the floor to allow maximum time before smoke inhalation clawed away at the backs of their throats, clung to their windpipes, filled their lungs like gas. Then he'd punched in the direct number to his old mucker, Gerry, and talked him all the way through it. The guy was a proper hero. He deserved to be walking around ambassadorial gardens like Field Marshall Montgomery.

"Steven, how are you feeling?" asked Margaret, softly. No longer hovering around the edges, but straight into the thick of it.

"I could do wi' a drink o' water. Me throat's like Gobi desert," said Stevo.

"I've phoned Back Road and they're bringing water for everyone. We'll have water to you very soon, Steven, very soon. Now, is there anything else you need? Anything, anything at all?"

"No ta, Margaret," said Stevo.

"Right. Good. Ah, Glenys, Kerry. Water's on its way..."

And she was off, getting stuck in. Like she used to. Overseeing circumstances in which altruism reigned and egos were forgotten.

I felt Helen looking over. She was sitting a few metres away, on the grass between Josh and Rosie, who had their heads bowed. Her arms around their shoulders, I could see her speaking kindly to them, empathically. But she was looking at me too, her eyes apologetic, seeking some reassurance for themselves. I could tell she was giving herself a hammering for letting the Project drag on too long. This wasn't her fault though. We'd all agreed that everything needed to be watertight, that the weight of evidence had to be enough to be decisive. Well, the weight of evidence was just about as decisive as it was going to get now. The sackable offence was as watertight as anything could be. Everyone had got out safely and the culprit was toast. Objective achieved. I was going to tell her that. And it wasn't Helen who'd left those two poor youths in charge, was it? Young adults, they might have been, but they were youths really. At least, they looked like youths now. I was going to ask Stevo if he was all right for a bit, whilst I went over to her, but then Josh started sobbing again and Helen had to turn all her attention back on to him and Rosie. Because that's what she's like. There's no judgement with her. She's not really into blaming people. If someone's suffering, and they need her help, she helps.

"Eh up, Stevo," I said, pulling him closer.

"Deborah's back," said Stevo.

I was like a wild cat cornered. The immediate instinct of anger and hatred paralysed me, as if I'd been showered in starch. Only my eyes moved. Watching. Watching. We were all still. All silently watching her.

She parked her car next to us, opposite the church hall. She slowly got out, mouth agape, looking like she was trying to comprehend the acrid aftermath, the smell of ash on the breeze. She took a step towards the burnt building, but then stumbled back slightly against the car bonnet, her new weekend hairdo full bodied, golden, dazzling against the blackness. She didn't move for a minute. Then she gradually started turning her head towards us. Slowly, slowly, tentatively, like a teetotaller waking up with an inexplicable hangover. Her tongue flickered across her lips, searching for moisture. She faced us, sweat beading her brow, hands shaking. She closed her mouth and swallowed deeply.

"But this is terrible," she said. "What happened here? Rosie, Josh, what happened here? Did everybody get out? Is everybody safe?"

"Everyone's safe, Deborah," said Helen.

"Everybody's safe, everybody's safe, everybody's safe," she said, like an incantation.

"New haircut, Deborah?" asked Margaret.

"Everybody's safe, everybody's safe, everybody's safe."

The miserable bastard was trying to reassure herself. But it was a bit like somebody grieving in a rocking chair; repeating, rocking, repeating, rocking, searching for solace, repeating, rocking. And I wanted her to suffer, then. I wanted to see her in pain. It was my kind of solace, seeing that. At that point I was even pissed off with Helen, letting her off the hook too easily. Reassuring her that no one had died. I didn't want her to know that. I wanted her to be thinking about it all the time, wondering if someone had been burnt alive in there. But I soon got back into it, seeing her there, starting to disintegrate, like the building she'd left behind. The bastard still wasn't finished trying to claw her way back out of it though.

"But Josh and Rosie, I am so proud of you. How often did we debate the importance of you taking on more responsibility? For the sake of your development. I've backed you in that. All the way. Right behind you, that's me. Isn't it, guys? That's why I've had the confidence to leave you in charge. I've always believed in you guys. I knew you could do it. And today, you've proved it. You have done a truly wonderful thing today. You've saved lives. And don't forget, *every* life is precious. You have saved lives today, guys, and nobody can ever take that away from you."

"It was Tony who saved us, saved everybody," said Rosie.

"What?" said Styles.

"It was Tony." said Josh.

She stared at Tony a moment, as if her preconceptions had been blown apart. It was like she was trying to piece it all back together. She wiped the sweat from her forehead, smearing a clammy hand through her new golden hairdo. Her face suddenly flushed hot crimson. She watched us unsteadily, her tongue erratically darting over her lips. She looked back at Tony, abject fear growing across her face. Her obsessive sense of control, the control she held over the students, Josh, Rosie, Margaret, us, herself, looked as though it was beginning to crumble, like mortar between bricks in the first tremor of an earthquake. I sensed her need for absolute control and self-possession was being shaken to the ground, as if by an act of God, her ego in the process of being blasted to smithereens. The sweat on her face glistened against the reddening of her skin. She visibly shook. She tried to swallow, but the back of her throat must have been like the desert. I imagined her tongue shrivelling like a snake's shed skin in the sand. And I watched her suffering. Every detail of it. An excitement, a fascination, gripped me. It drew me in. As if I was right up to her face. Seeing the fear behind her eyes, smelling the aridity of her breath, living inside the tremors as they tore up the control freak and its ego. It was like a first shot of heroin. One hit and I'm in the throes of addiction. She seemed to stagger slightly, steadying herself against the bonnet of her car. She was sweating profusely, shaking uncontrollably, I thought she was going to puke. And her breath was shortening, gasping. Gasping for the thick acrid air.

"Quick! Quick!" shouted Helen, alerting a paramedic.

We were told not to get too close, to give the lady some space.

"Panic attack," said the paramedic.

The paramedic sat her down, asked her name, spoke reassuringly to her. She told her to try to control her breathing. She told her that she understood. The paramedic was sympathetic and caring. She was like Helen. But the symptoms worsened. And the paramedic said she'd like to take the lady to the hospital, as a precautionary measure. And the paramedic said it might be beneficial to the lady if somebody close to her could accompany her in the ambulance. Because having somebody there close to the lady might help her to calm down. It might give her some reassurance and support.

Helen wanted to go. But I wanted to go more. I could still see the terror on Styles' face, and I wanted to go more. The paramedic and the driver helped her into the ambulance, got her to lie down on the slightly inclined trolley, made her as comfortable as possible. And when the paramedic was attending to her I climbed onboard. Helen was just outside the doors, looking intently up at me. I bent down and we kissed and the gentle wave spread slowly to my fingertips. And as I closed the door, she was looking up at me again, eyes wide, deeply attentive. In the ambulance I sat down close to Styles, gazing at the ceiling, and those attentive eyes were still fixed in my head. I only snapped out of it when the driver fired up the engine.

We rumbled steadily along the streets. I stared at the dull, green, cramped ambulance interior, the prosaic medical equipment. I listened to Styles' laboured breathing, to the panic heating up inside her. It drew me in and I found myself standing and moving, so I was right behind her, my stomach brushing against the top of her new golden hairdo every time we hit a bump in the road. I looked down into her face, watched her lying there, gripping the trolley like the victim of a fit, her hands violently shaking, the redness in her cheeks and neck hot with suffering. I smiled. The paramedic was standing beside her, stroking her arm. She shot me a glance. Then she turned back to Styles.

"Deborah. Ok, Deborah, now I want you to listen to me. Everything is going to be fine, but you need to listen to me now. I'm going to help you control your breathing. Okay, Deborah? We need to give you back some control."

The paramedic tried to get her to breathe in for "one... two" and out for "one... two." She kept repeating it, "In... one... two... out... one... two."

But poor old Deborah was having none of it. She was out of control. Not a vestige remained. All drained away. Her life, a drought. Pure panic. And this for one who needed absolute control, at all times, over everything. The poor old girl's ego had been blasted to smithereens. I could hear her gasping for breath. I could hear the panic inside her. I could see the sweat rolling off her face. I could see the fear behind her eyes.

"What's your name, love?" the paramedic asked me.

"Mmm?" I mumbled, irritated at the interruption.

"Your name?"

"Pete."

"Pete, I think Deborah could use your help now."

"What?"

"She could use someone who's close to her. Speak to her, Pete. Reassure her. Hold her hand."

"You what?"

"Hold her hand. Firmly, but gently."

The ambulance leaned around a long corner.

"It's all right, Deborah," said the paramedic. "It's all right, love. Come on, Pete, look lively."

I took hold of one of Styles' shaking, sweaty hands.

"Stroke it," said the paramedic.

"Eh?" I said.

"Stroke it. Softly. Stroke it."

The ambulance rumbled steadily along the streets.

"All right, Deborah. It's all right, darling," said the paramedic. "Just try to control your breathing. Breathe in... one... two... breathe out... one... two..."

I looked down at Styles. She was gulping at the air, searching for it with her arid mouth, flickering at it with her 'shrivelled' tongue.

"She's still struggling, Pete. You see those brown paper bags to your left? Pass me one, please... Cor, they didn't build you for speed, did they, love? It's all right, Deborah, everything's going to be fine. In... one... two... out... one... two."

Now I was bending over the new golden hairdo, a brown paper bag in one hand, Styles' clammy hand in the other. I could still hear her gasping, panicking. I watched the paramedic helping. Not judging, not blaming. That was her job, her vocation, the reason she'd got into the whole shebang. Not to judge, not to blame, but to help. Not to hate. If someone's suffering and they need her help, she helps.

"Pass me the bag then, Pete," said the paramedic.

So I'm standing over Styles, with the bag in my hand. And I'm looking down at her, lying there. I'm looking into her eyes, seeing the fear behind them. I'm watching her shake and gasp and gulp and sweat. And now I'm sweating.

"Okay, Deborah," says the paramedic. "We're going to use a paper bag to help you breathe, to stop you hyperventilating. We'll place it gently over your mouth and nose, and you just keep breathing, as we've been practicing. Can you do that for us? There's nothing to worry about. It will help calm you down, that's all, darling. Pete, pass me the bag."

I'm watching Styles gripping the sides of the trolley, violently shaking.

"What are you doing, Pete? Do *you* want to hold the bag for her?"

I'm levelling my eyes at the paramedic, dead steady, dead straight. I'm feeling my head slowly nodding.

"Okay, that's fine. Perhaps she'll find it more reassuring from a close friend. Give me her hand and I'll talk her through it."

And now I'm moving Styles' sweaty hand mechanically towards the paramedic. The paramedic is holding her hand. The paramedic is talking her through her breathing. I'm opening the paper bag with my own sweaty hands.

"Now, Pete, when I tell you, hold the bag over her mouth and nose. Deborah, just keep breathing in... one... two... out...

one... two. Okay, darling? This is going to help you. Right, Pete, place the bag gently over her mouth and nose and hold it there."

But I'm listening intently to Styles' arid gasping. And now my face is right over hers. And a drop of my own sweat splashes onto her cheek.

"Pete, what are you waiting for?" says the paramedic.

I'm looking into Styles' dried up mouth.

"She needs you to do it now, Pete."

I'm watching her tongue lick the air.

"Put the bag over her nose and mouth."

I'm thinking, that tongue's shrivelling, like a snake's dead skin in the sand.

"Right, give me the bag," says the paramedic.

But I'm thinking, 'that's my job.' And now I'm placing the bag firmly over Styles' nose and mouth. I'm using both hands, to get a decent grip.

"That's it, Pete. Not too tight. Gently. Okay, Deborah, in... one... two... out... one... two."

And my hold is beginning to tighten slightly. I'm not intending it. I don't intend it. But I can feel the bone in her nose and the teeth under her cheeks.

"It's all right, Deborah," says the paramedic. "This should help. Not too tight, Pete."

And now I've stopped listening to the paramedic. I'm looking at Styles' eyes, staring out at me from above a paper bag. I wonder if they're widening a bit. I can see the fear behind them. It intrigues me, seeing that.

Then sweat gets in my eyes. I clench them shut, trying to

soak up the sweat. But I get this image behind my eyes. And I blink, and I keep blinking, and this image is still there, every time I blink. This image of a woman looking up at me, her eyes deeply attentive. Every time I blink, she's there. Then I look into *Styles'* eyes once more. But they seem blurred now. They blur, they blur. And, for a moment, they're different eyes. Not fearful, but attentive.

I snap out of it when the ambulance hits a bump in the road.

"That's still a bit tight, Pete," says the paramedic.

Styles is looking into my eyes.

"Deborah, in... one... two... out... one... two," says the paramedic.

I am looking into Styles' eyes. But I can see the fear behind them.

"In... one... two... out... one... two.

She is looking into my eyes.

"That's better, Pete. Nice and gently, love."

I am looking into her eyes.

"In... one... two... out... one... two."

She is looking into my eyes.

"In... one... two... out... one... two."

Lightning Source UK Ltd.
Milton Keynes UK
UKOW052204120213

206210UK00001B/2/P